FBI CASE: QUANTICO KILL

Steve Gladis

Disclaimer: This is a work of fiction. Names, characters, places, and incidents are the product of the author's imagination or are used fictitiously. Any resemblance to actual events, locales, or persons, living or dead, is coincidental.

Publisher: SGLP

ISBN: 978-0-9891314-7-6 (paperback)
ISBN: 978-0-9891314-8-3 (e-book)

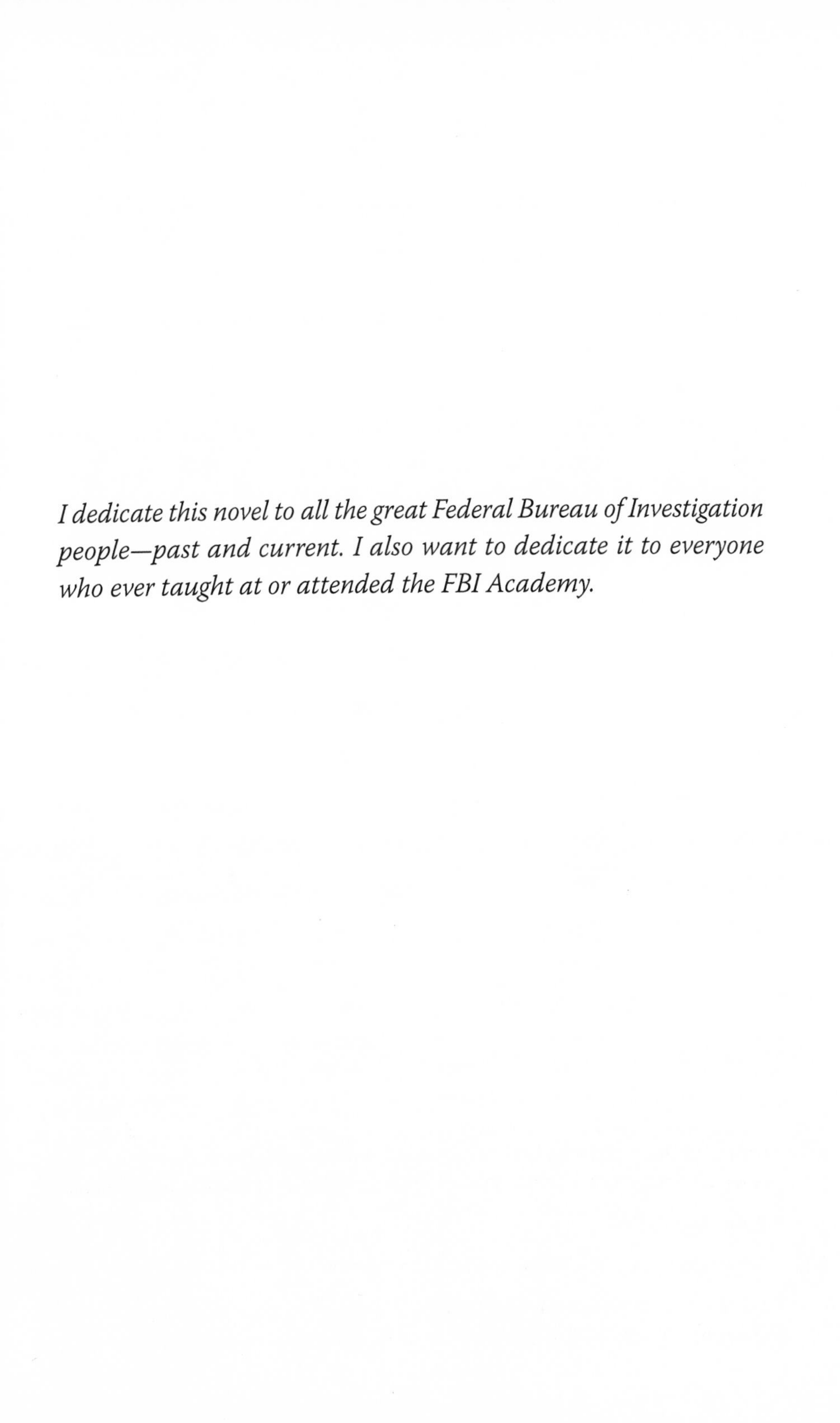

I dedicate this novel to all the great Federal Bureau of Investigation people—past and current. I also want to dedicate it to everyone who ever taught at or attended the FBI Academy.

1
FBI ACADEMY
Monday, September 15

The runner's gait was strong but fluid, especially for a guy who looked more like a linebacker than a marathoner. He'd run this pine-forested trail many times in the solitude of the early morning, knowing that for one hour, he would be completely alone and free. He knew the trail's twists and turns, its ups and downs—its personality. His stained green FBI National Academy T-shirt stuck to his black, glistening skin for dear life on this still-humid fall morning as he sped along this path. It crested a slight hill near Lunga Reservoir, about a half mile from the Academy gym, where he'd departed just 10 minutes before. The runner's routine started between 5 AM and 5:15 AM each morning to get in his daily 5-mile run before breakfast and classes at the FBI's National Academy.

And today, he was on schedule as he ran down the wooded path. When the familiar blind corner came into view, he adjusted his speed to give the sharp angle in the path the respect it deserved. As he leaned back to decelerate a bit, he caught a flash of movement from the very pine tree that had created the turn in the first place. Startled, he stopped so fast that he nearly lost his balance, kicking up the dirt and pine needles at his feet. At that precise moment, three black-hooded figures erupted from behind the tree.

Two of the figures were football-tackle large and wielded aluminum bats, the first swing of which crashed into the runner's right knee with such force that the sound of breaking bone and aluminum pinging ricocheted off the nearby trees. As the runner sank to his knees in pain, the third attacker, smaller than the other two, leveled a ferocious swing and connected with the runner's head. Sickening melon thuds punctuated the quiet morning air. In less than three minutes, the runner lay lifeless on the path overlooking the serene water of the reservoir.

Almost an hour later, a second runner negotiated the same trail. This runner was tall, lean, and wore a yellow T-shirt that read **FBI ACADEMY STAFF** in bold black letters across the back. He also tried to negotiate the blind corner by slowing down, but not soon enough. He slipped on a pair of bloody, torn running shorts and landed in a coagulated pool of blood that had settled on the trail. The ground looked like it had been assaulted in a terrible struggle. With that much blood, there had to be a body close by. He rose up on his knees to look around and saw a tree about 30 yards away with something swinging from it. His stomach lurched.

He got up, wiping off as much blood as possible, and approached the tree. A naked, bloodied African American man's body hung from a rope. The body twisted off the reservoir in the early morning breeze, and suddenly the runner could see a swastika carved on his chest. He fished his phone from his shorts pocket, but there was no service. He took off running and didn't stop until he reached an open field and a few bars of service. Breathing heavily, he dialed the main Academy number. "This is Special Agent Ford. Give me the duty agent. We have an emergency."

2
THE RESPONSE
Monday, September 15

Like the stock market, the FBI doesn't react; it overreacts. Most duty agents would have panicked and called Ralph Pelham, the agent in charge of the Academy, but the duty agent on call that morning had been around the block a few times. He knew how crazy it got, so he took a few leveling breaths, called the security chief, and told him the situation.

"Get over to the scene fast with a few security folks, confirm what's happened and how bad the situation is, and call me back immediately."

In less than 10 minutes, the security chief called back. "Yeah, it's bad. Holy shit! Black male, hung—lynched—with a swastika carved in his chest. Call the Assistant Director ASAP and—" That was all the duty agent heard because he immediately cut the line and dialed the Assistant Director.

Within the hour, there were a hundred people at the scene and more on the way—agents, cops, National Academy students, and anyone legitimately on the Base who had heard about the murder. Even the Hostage Rescue Team (HRT) sent a contingent to cordon off the area and collect intel in case it was a national security issue or even the slightest chance of a follow-up murder.

The Bureau had emergency operations plans for such significant events. Still, they happened so infrequently at FBI facilities that agents and first responders acted as if no plan existed, creating a response out of whole cloth every time. Today was no different. It was wildly disorganized because the Academy was more than a few steps from the reality of an operational functioning of an FBI field office. Indeed, while the faculty and staff were, as a group, the best-educated folks in the FBI, they were not the best investigators. In fact, they might have been the worst.

When Ralph Pelham rolled up in his new, fully equipped Ford Explorer, he was met by his faithful deputy, Jack Eller. "Who's heading up the investigation, and where's the ops center?" Pelham asked.

Jack looked at him like a deer in the headlights and said, "I guess, for now, I am…and well, this is as good a place for a CP."

Pelham nearly lost it. "Get the lab guys out here, have HRT set up a command-post tent with comms, food, trackers, and dogs. Notify the base commander of the Marine Corps, Prince William PD, and the State Troopers. Get this shit show organized now! Jesus H. Christ, we have a Black officer lynched on our property, and we respond like Andy Mayberry and Barney Fife."

"Who, sir?"

"Just get your ass in gear." With that, Pelham stalked off to the scene of the murder. When he got to the clearing overlooking the tree where the body swung slowly in the morning breeze, he was surprised at how viscerally he reacted to the sight. He'd seen a lot of death and destruction in his career, but this was malicious and purposely horrific. And on Academy grounds! Sacrilegious. He strode up to the group of 15 uniformed officers and agents from the Academy standing around. "Who's in charge of this scene?" He barked. Everyone looked at each other with a kind of blank stare. Finally, one brave soul spoke up. "Sir, we were waiting for the lab guys to show up and trying not to disturb the scene."

"Any of you have experience in the lab?" One lonely agent reluctantly pushed his right hand into the air. "Good. You're in charge for now until the forensic folks arrive. Preserve the scene and take pictures of everything that looks relevant with your cell phones."

"Yes, sir," the new crime scene chief said with the same conviction as a teen who'd been put in charge of his three siblings while his parents left for the grocery store. Before he could say anything else, Pelham felt his phone buzz. "What?"

"Sir, two things," said his harried-sounding deputy. "One, the media just turned up. And two, the Director wants you to call her ASAP."

3
A POSH HOTEL
Monday, September 15

The suites at The Walsh Los Angeles International Hotel were spacious and well-appointed, looking more like luxury apartments. In suite 704, the oriental rug was bright and intricate, and the fine leather furniture smelled authentic and expensive. On one of the leather-wing chairs, a dark blue Armani suit jacket had been unceremoniously tossed, and the suit's matching pants connected the chair to the floor like a conduit. A forest green silk dress and open-toed 3-inch cream heels lay on the floor not far from the leather chair. Closer to the king-sized bed on a smaller leather chair lay a pale blue monogrammed shirt, white silk boxers with fine black polka dots, and a lonely black knee-length sock. A bright floral matching set of tiny panties and a bra lay not two feet away, marking the path to the king-sized destination. The bed itself was a sculpture of covers comingled with sheets and dented pillows. It did not look as though much sleeping had happened.

The digital bedside clock read 6:30 AM. Next to the clock was a silver ice bucket with an empty bottle of Dom Perignon and an empty Tiffany bracelet box. In the background, the shower sounded like tropical rain. The bathroom was embarrassingly large. The shower head spewed a torrent of steaming water and was perched like a low cloud a foot over the heads of the two entwined figures still at the business of love making. The man was maybe 6'4" and the woman a foot shorter, but he was most accommodating as the steam billowed and fogged up the glass playground. Water, steam, and soft moaning.

Suddenly the distinctive "dun DUN" of the *Law and Order* theme rang out from his cell phone. The sound froze him in place on his knees. "Shit," he said as he looked up at the object of his affection, and then bolted naked from the shower to the bedroom and picked up the phone on the 5th ring. He would let only one ringtone interrupt a moment like that. He took a deep breath, "Nathaniel Croft."

On the other end of the phone, a male voice said, "Inspector Croft, wait one for the Director."

Still built like the collegiate rower he had once been, Nathaniel stood almost at attention and pulled a sheet off the bed to wrap around himself as he pushed his longish black hair away from his bright blue eyes. By now, his blond companion, at 35, a full decade his junior, was draped in a towel that drooped below one firm breast. She stood by the open bathroom door and raised a perfectly shaped eyebrow at her runaway lover. He grimaced and mouthed the words FBI DIRECTOR. She nodded and retreated into the bathroom to get a real shower, with soap this time. He watched as she dropped her towel and disappeared back into the steam until a crisp voice sounded in his ear.

"Nathaniel?"

"Yes, Director. And how are you this fine day?"

Judge Ann Greenburg sat ramrod in her leather executive judge chair, familiar and comfortable to her as a former federal judge for 15 years before she was appointed Director. At 5'11" in her customary 3-inch heels, she towered over many of her male subordinates, a move that, like everything else she did, was strategic. She ran a hand through her lightly graying blonde hair as she reviewed the file before her. Her ears perked up at a sound coming from Nathaniel's end of the conversation.

"Where are you? What's that sound in the background?"

He turned around and looked through the open bathroom door at the gorgeous blond all soaped up in the shower.

"Don't ever let them tell you it never rains in Southern California."

"That so?"

"Director, would I ever lie to you?"

"Let's not go there, Nathaniel. Listen, a detective from Detroit, Mohammed Rasheed, was found murdered at the Academy early this morning."

"A National Academy student?"

"Yes, AND an African American AND a Muslim. AND he was found naked, hanging from a tree. AND had a swastika carved on his chest."

"Lynched and cut? Messy. Someone was trying to make a statement. A Muslim? Any terrorist connection?"

"Don't know the exact motive yet, but the swastika certainly sends a strong signal, almost too conspicuous. Congressman Morrison from Michigan is all over me about possible religious retaliation. And why we don't have any Black agents on the case? And that Black-agent class action suit against the Bureau last year only fuels the fire. I want you to take over the investigation today and make it right."

He looked at the blonde and smiled, "But Director, I have SO much unfinished business out here. I—"

"I'll reassign someone else to the LA inspection. See you in my office tomorrow."

Nathaniel sighed. Tomorrow meant he had at least the rest of the morning in LA. He dropped the sheet and headed towards the shower. He intended to make the most of it.

After the Director hung up, she turned toward her assistant, listening on the extension and taking notes. "Check today's weather in LA for me."

4
TWO AIRPORTS

Tuesday, September 16

Nathaniel landed at Cleveland's Hopkins Airport on a United Airlines flight from Los Angeles. He was the last to emerge from the plane, chatting to the two flight attendants as he emerged from the walkway into the bustling terminal. Tall and decked out in his tailored Armani—a dark blue pinstripe this time, with a red silk tie and pale blue shirt with 14-carat gold FBI cuff links—Nathaniel towered over the two attendants.

Nathaniel looked around and spotted his first field-training agent and mentor from twenty years ago, Charlie Thompson, who had been watching this familiar extraverted ballet between Nathaniel and whoever was nearby. Charlie had shepherded Nathaniel through his first year as a special agent. It was a mentoring job, only given to senior agents with patience and a willingness to teach the subtleties of the work: How to treat the mucky-mucks and those on the lowest rung of society with dignity. He remembered when Nathaniel showed up the first day dressed like he was modeling for the next issue of G.Q. It was raining, and they had to search for a fugitive in the attic of a nasty old row house. When they got through, Nathaniel looked like he'd been in a fight with a vacuum cleaner and lost. That's when Charlie taught him about wearing a "rain suit." That was FBI code for wearing an old suit on rainy days or when you knew you'd be hunting for fugitives in dirty basements or dusty attics.

At 56, Charlie had grown thin, almost gaunt, and now he wore wire-rimmed glasses that aged him even further. As always, he had a book with him. Lately, he'd been reading David Baldacci's Memory Man. He loved the character of Amos Decker, a pro-football player, for precisely one day, who got his bell rung, was hospitalized for months, and then could recall anything he'd ever seen, unlike Charlie at this point in his life. He wrote down essential things in a green notebook in his upper right suit jacket pocket. Like most right-handed agents, his upper left suit jacket pocket was reserved for his FBI credentials—the most important possession of any agent. There isn't an agent in the history of the FBI who hasn't stood in front of a mirror practicing repeatedly extracting those "creds" with one hand, flipping them open and saying, "hello, I'm Mary or Jack Smith with the FBI."

Nathaniel made eye contact with Charlie, and as he got within striking distance, Nathaniel stuck out his right hand, grabbing Charlie's and pulling him in for a bro-hug.

"Charlie, how the hell are you, buddy?"

"Great to see you, Nate.."

"Inspector Croft," he said as he winked.

"Right!"

They headed down the concourse. Charlie looked at his former protégé and asked, "So, where are you headed now?"

"Back to Quantico. Hey, you want a coffee? I'm still on LA time," said Nathaniel as he spotted a Starbucks.

"Do they even have plain coffee?"

Nathaniel laughed. "Yeah, but I'm gonna get you an Americano. It'll be fresher."

"Whatever you say, Sport. As long as you do the ordering."

Charlie watched as Nathaniel approached the counter. He gave a big smile to the middle-aged Black woman behind the register, who looked like she'd been on her feet too long in a tedious job to be charmed by anyone. Nathaniel leaned in slightly, made steady eye contact, and left his wallet on the counter. It didn't take a body language expert to see what he was doing. When she handed him back his card, the woman smiled at Nathaniel, who winked in return and dropped a $5 bill in the tip jar. The interaction had taken only three minutes, and Charlie marveled, not for the first time, at Nathaniel's off-the-charts people skills. He'd spotted it right away when Nathaniel was still a recruit. He was more polished now, but the boyish charm remained. Charlie watched him walk over to the milk station and add half and half and a single sugar to Charlie's coffee. Twenty years since they'd worked together, and Nathaniel still remembered how he took his coffee. Charlie smiled.

"Let's grab a seat over there," Nathaniel said, pointing to an empty boarding area. I'm just laying over for an hour." He handed Charlie his coffee. "Still half and half and one sugar, right?"

Charlie laughed. "You got it." He took a sip. "Hey, this is better than their usual coffee. What'd you call it again?"

"An Americano. It's espresso with hot water. It tastes like regular coffee, but the shots are pulled fresh, so it's better than whatever's been sitting in the coffee maker."

"Uh-huh. I'm still a Dunkin man, but this is pretty good."

After they sat down, Nathaniel turned to Charlie and said, "I caught that lynching case at Quantico."

Charlie whistled. "Good luck, kid. Shit, a lynching at the Academy—it's blasphemy! I wish I could've seen the expression on the Emperor of Quantico's face—Mr. Fidelity, Bravery, and whatever...."

"Yep. That's why I need your help, Charlie. Pelham will hand me a turd and demand that I polish it with the help of his lackeys. None of whom I trust."

Charlie looked at Nathaniel. His expression changed instantly when he got where this was going.

"Wait a fuckin' minute. NO way, Nathaniel. You're not Pullin' me into another pile of crap."

Nathaniel put up his hand like a cop stopping traffic. "Look, Charlie, they've got 50 agents working on this case, stepping over each other. I can't work that way. You know me."

"No way. No fucking way. I stepped off that treadmill last year when Dianne died. Cancer…" he paused as his voice caught and cast his eyes down. "Look, I'm retiring next year. Mandatory."

Nathaniel put his hand on Charlie's shoulder.

"You know how sorry I am about Dianne—she was such a special woman and like a second mother to me here in Cleveland as a first-office agent."

"I can't. Besides, my mother's here in a nursing home."

"Charlie, last time we spoke, you told me she's in and out of consciousness. We can get her moved. Besides, it's already a done deal."

Charlie flashed a look of surprise more than anger. "Done deal?"

Nathaniel reached into his jacket pocket and handed Charlie a copy of an email from the Office of the Director. Charlie read it, looked at Nathaniel, reread it, and said, "Son of a bitch! You had me reassigned to Quantico? The Goddamn Bureau's halfway house for naval gazers—to work for you?" He paused and declared, "Screw it. I'll retire."

Nathaniel glanced at his Rolex, then got serious and looked at Charlie with his piercing blue eyes and asked, "To do WHAT, exactly? Rot in Cleveland? Drink yourself to death? The orders stand. See you Monday at Quantico or invite me to your retirement party."

Nathaniel stood up, took a few steps away, then turned around and walked right up to Charlie in front of a bunch of people who had started populating the waiting area, hugged him, and planted a big, noisy kiss on his cheek. He winked at Charlie and said, "I love you, man!"

"You ever do that again, Nathaniel, and I will retire, I swear to God."

Nathaniel walked again toward a gate heading for DC, pivoted back, and said, "See you Monday, Charlie! And for the record, it's Nathaniel now, not Nate."

"You'll always be Nate to me, Sport."

Nathaniel blew him a kiss. Charlie threw him the finger.

In the late evening, Ronald Regan National Airport gleams like a jewel. Nathaniel looked out at the cityscape as his plane glided over the Potomac toward this shrine to the former Hollywood actor and 34th President of the United States. He thought of all the politicians and power brokers drawn to this city like metal shavings to a strong magnet. He thought of his father, who regularly visited this political mecca when Nathaniel was a kid. He'd spend a week, buy support in Congress for his bank's investments, and then fly back to Logan Airport and limo to his brownstone on Mount Vernon Street in Boston's elite Beacon Hill. He taught Nathaniel all about power, so Nathaniel preferred the West Coast and went to Stanford, not Harvard, which bothered his father no end.

When Nathaniel landed and walked up the ramp to the terminal, he was greeted by two young FBI Agents. One agent approached him and said, "Inspector Croft, I'm Special Agent Morris, and this is Special Agent Rubinsky. We'll escort you to the resident agent's office." Nathaniel smiled and nodded.

As the federal-agent caravan approached a glass door with the FBI seal etched in frosted glass in the center of it, special agent Morris held the door for the Inspector.

Once inside, Agent Morris directed Nathaniel to a small conference room. Seated at the head of the mahogany conference table was an impeccably dressed, very tall African American, a senior partner of an exclusive DC law firm. Terry Jamison was reading the Wall Street Journal and was slow to look up from his article.

Nathaniel spoke first in deference. “Mr. Jamison, I'm sorry you had to wait. Our plane—well, I'm Nathaniel Croft,” he said as he offered his hand. Jamison looked up warily from his paper. Without standing, he cautiously shook Nathaniel's hand and said, “Terry Jamison. So, what's this all about? Why exactly am I sitting here and not at home? All I got was Bureau mumbo jumbo about some big case.” His deep baritone was awash in suspicion. Nathaniel also noted he had the precise diction standard with trial lawyers. Jamison was not a man at ease.

“The Director's put me in charge of the FBI Academy hate crime case.”

“You mean the lynching .”

“Yes, sir. It will be all over the news in the morning. A Black Detroit police officer was found lynched in the woods with a swastika carved into his chest. And Congressman Morrison from Michigan has demanded that we have an African American on the case. So, I'd like your help.”

Terry looked at Nathaniel and said, “Inspector, do you know who I am?” By the end of the sentence, disbelief had slipped into icy sarcasm.

“Yes, sir. You're Terrence M. Jamison, 48 years old, born in Anacostia, one of DC's poorest neighborhoods, raised by a single mother, Walker Jamison. Your younger brother Ricky died of a drug overdose. A Metropolitan DC cop and Big Brother took you under his wing. You attended Ballou High in Anacostia and entered the Math/Science special program. Graduated with honors, got into Howard, then Georgetown Law. Became an FBI agent ten years ago. Served as a major complainant in a class action discrimination suit against the FBI five years ago before leaving for private practice with Williams, Jeffords, and Schwartz. That's the short version. I could go on.”

Jamison looked impressed, then nodded slowly. “Just wanted to make sure. But frankly, I have no interest in helping the FBI look like they're racially sensitive after proving they are not."

"We'll pay your daily rate. At the end of the three months, you can walk. A straight business deal."

"No thanks," Terry said as he stood and walked toward the door.

Then Nathaniel posed a question to the back of Jamison's head, "Remember Ralph Pelham when he was the Unit Chief of New Agents Training? He convened the new agents' review board—the NARB—to get you dumped from new agents training on an allegation of cheating."

Terry paused but did not turn around. Nathaniel could see Terry's shoulders rise and fall as he breathed intensely. Images of that awful period in his life had to be flashing across Terry's brain like a disorienting strobe light. The allegations of cheating, the insinuations without proof, the pompous, disparaging tone of Pelham's voice as he recommended Terry's immediate dismissal from the FBI Academy—all flashed before his eyes instantly.

"Yes. What about Pelham?" Jamison spit out.

"Now he's the Agent in Charge of the entire FBI Academy."

"I see that the good-ole-white-boys club's still alive and well," Jamison said, moving again toward the door.

Then with precise calculation of an NFL quarterback, Nathaniel threw a Hail Mary pass. "If you don't help me, Pelham will assign some Bureau-loyal Uncle Tom to my task force."

Terry stopped short like he'd been slapped in the face. His voice stayed even, but Nathaniel saw his shoulders tense. "You're out of line, Inspector. I should report your comments to the Director."

"Go ahead. I get a free trip back to LA, and Pelham whitewashes the investigation."

By now, Terry had turned and looked directly into Nathaniel's eyes. Silence for seconds that felt like minutes. Terry blinked first. "Let me think about it for a few days."

"Can't. We start tomorrow. So if I see you in Ralph Pelham's office at 9 AM, I'll know your answer. By the way, Ralph has no idea about my invitation to you. Could be fun to see his face when you arrive, " Nathaniel said.

Terry turned back to the door, which Agent Morris held. He smiled quickly, but Nathaniel could not see his face.

"See you when I see you."

"Fair enough. I'll have an agent take you home."

"No need, I have a driver waiting," said Terry as he swept out.

5
THE FBI ACADEMY

Tuesday, September 16

Before his brutal murder, Mohammed Rasheed had been an elite officer attending the FBI National Academy. Known as the "Harvard of Law Enforcement," the FBI Academy represents the epicenter for the FBI and key law enforcement officers from the US and worldwide and as a law enforcement research center. Home base to the famed Hostage Rescue Team, the Behavioral Sciences Unit, the FBI Laboratory, and much more, the Academy has generated many worldwide tactical, psychological, and biological innovations for law enforcement.

Operated by the FBI's Training Division, the Academy occupies 547 acres, still just a fraction of Marine Corps Base Quantico, which spreads over 59,000 acres. The FBI Academy also houses the FBI National Academy—law enforcement's premier police executive training program. Often confused with the FBI Academy, the FBI National Academy Program was established in 1935 during Prohibition to ensure nationwide standardization and professionalism of law enforcement training.

Ten weeks in duration, four classes a year of 250 elite officers from around the world attend the FBI National Academy, whose academic courses are accredited by the prestigious University of Virginia. Officers must be leaders of local, state, or sheriff's departments to attend. Military police and law enforcement agencies from the US and globally also apply to the rigorous program involving academics, firearms, physical training, and connections worldwide that last a lifetime.

The entrance to the FBI Academy bears the Federal Bureau of Investigation's motto: Fidelity, Bravery, Integrity. And no one espoused those values more often or articulately than the Director of the Academy, Ralph Pelham. Often in front of a press conference such as the rather harried one he'd most recently given to explain the FBI's response to Rasheed's murder, Pelham would remind the media by punctuating his comments with those values. He affixed these values to his emails just below his signature. He'd repeated it at the end of his speeches so often that staff would mouth it as a subtle mocking gesture. As a strategic result, he'd become the brand owner of those values, exactly what he'd planned.

At 56, Ralph Pelham had become one of the longest-tenured of the nearly 25 Assistant Directors in the FBI, each of whom headed key divisions like terrorism, intelligence, technology, and criminal investigations. Tall, athletic, and a former practicing assistant US Attorney from Richmond, Virginia, he ran his office like a courtroom: stately, formal, and by the book. Before his Academy assignment, Pelham had served as a special agent in Detroit, a supervisory special agent in Cleveland, a counterterrorism Unit Chief at FBI Headquarters, and a Special Agent in Charge of the Jacksonville Field Office. He was also one of the few Special Agents in Charge of a field office with a law degree and a Ph.D., which landed him the top job at the Academy. So when Ann Greenburg ascended as the Director after being a federal Judge in Jacksonville, where she initially met the upwardly mobile Ralph Pelham, he became one of her first appointments.

Pelham's office was like a vast windshield on the Academy and the entrance to this law enforcement fortress. Like a king in his castle, Pelham would sit behind his massive desk and look out his floor-to-ceiling windows to see any official caravans of the Director or other dignitaries who visited his domain. He even kept a pair of binoculars in the upper-right-hand drawer of his desk to size up significant guests before they entered. But today, Pelham watched as a lone car parked in a visitor slot. A US Marine emerged, immediately recognizable by his ramrod-straight posture, even if he hadn't been in uniform. He walked with purpose toward the front door of the Academy and beneath the FBI seal.

Several minutes later, Sergeant Major Avery T. Wilson was escorted into the inner sanctum by Pelham's executive assistant. At 5' 8," Wilson was shorter than Pelham by 5 inches. However, his erect posture and crisp Marine Corps uniform made him look taller. Four rows of bright ribbons emblazoned the upper left chest of his knife-sharp creased summer-service shirt. The most prestigious valor awards sat at the top of any Marine's ribbons. In Wilson's case, a blue ribbon with a single white vertical stripe was perched in the center. The Navy Cross was the second-highest medal awarded for extreme bravery to anyone in the Marine Corps. The Navy Cross bowed only to the Medal of Honor.

The two men shook hands and then sat in the two leather chairs in a conversation nook near the window overlooking the lawn.

"Ralph, thanks for taking the time during what has to be a shit storm. I know you're busy these days with the lynchin' and all."

"That's putting it mildly, Avery. My phone's been ringing off the hook. Frankly, it's a pleasure to sit down and ignore it briefly."

"So, let me cut to the chase. I've come to ask for a favor for the General."

"Shoot," Pelham said, as close to a joke as possible.

"The General wants to put someone on your murder task force as liaison."

Pelham stiffened a bit. "I understand, Avery, but we'll keep you up to speed on the case. We'll brief you and the General whenever he needs an update."

Wilson leaned forward and locked eyes with Pelham. "Ralph, the General's real touchy these days. You know he's prepping for his Senate hearings to become the next Commandant. And you know how pesky they can be. The Senate hearing's on September 29, in just thirteen days. This murder, being on the base he commands, could muck up the hearings—if you know what I mean. But if you can put a Marine on the taskforce as a personal favor for me, it'd save me a big ass chewin'."

"Avery, I will certainly see what I can do. But the case's being turned over to an inspector," Pelham said as he winced. "The Director handpicked this guy, and he's a tight-circle kind of guy. Fiercely independent."

Wilson leaned even closer. "What else can ya' tell me about him?

"Name's Nathaniel Croft. Smart. Phillips Exeter, then Stanford. Father was a big-time banker and kingmaker in Boston before he died. And years later, when his mother died, she left Nathaniel the entire estate—and we're talking an estate—properties, investments, you name it. Frankly, I'm not sure why he's even working at a job, especially for the Bureau —he sure doesn't need the money. And he can be, ah, difficult. Pain in the ass, to put it bluntly."

"Maybe you could put someone on the task force now—before he even gets here?"

"He's probably going to dump my entire initial response team anyway. Start from scratch with his own crew. That's his M.O. We're not exactly friends either. But if the Commandant happened to call the Director—say even today—that could change things."

Wilson smiled and winked at Pelham. "I think we can arrange that."

6
THE TWO QUANTICOS

Tuesday, September 16

At 55, Lieutenant General Wesley Mathers looked like a poster Marine. Tall and broad-shouldered, he towered over almost everyone he'd ever met. Growing up, his father had constantly corrected his slouching posture, which is why Wesley sat so ramrod stiff today. As a three-star general, he commanded the Marine Corps Combat Development Command, the West Point of the Marine Corps. He was responsible for the training and education of new lieutenants as well as generals. The commanding general of Quantico also serves as the Deputy Commandant of the Marine Corps—the successor to the throne.

Mathers lived in Quarters 1 at Quantico. Built in 1920, the two-story Dutch Colonial, white with black shutters, sat regally on a hill overlooking Neville Road. A majestic palace for the Prince of the Marine Corps, it was on the National Register of Historic Places. For the past two weeks, Mathers had been working from home, nestled in his oak-lined study, to concentrate on his upcoming Senate hearing. Arranged neatly on his massive mahogany desk sat three thick black briefing binders.

Mathers' aide escorted Avery Wilson into the study. Wilson, who had served in combat in Iraq and Afghanistan with Mathers, revered his commander and knew the General's inner sanctum well. The library was a shrine to his Marine Corps service and was filled with plaques, pictures, and art representing every clime and place in which Mathers had served since he was a new lieutenant. He was surrounded by his career, from the photo of him graduating from The Basic School as a second lieutenant to being sworn in as a brigadier general and having his first star pinned on by his wife.

Wilson walked in a straight line, pivoted precisely at a right angle to position himself squarely in front of the general's desk at ridged attention—not saluting because Marines traditionally don't salute indoors with their covers (hats) off. Otherwise, he would have popped a razor-sharp salute.

Mathers said, "C'mon, Avery, at ease, buddy. So, how'd it go with the FBI?" He motioned Wilson to the leather chair in front of his desk.

Wilson sat and said, "Well, I talked to Ralph Pelham. He danced me around the floor about putting a Marine on the task force."

Mathers put down his pen, sat up straighter, and focused his stern gaze on Wilson. He breathed, expanding his broad chest, which supported six rows of ribbons topped by the Silver Star. "Goddamn it, Avery, a Black man gets lynched on a United States Marine Corps Base."

"Yes sir, terrible thing, sir."

"On my watch, Avery. My watch. And all the negative press that comes with this kind of crap. It could seriously cloud the hearings and make me—I mean the Corps—look bad."

"Due respect, sir, I'll refer any reporter to the FBI's public information office."

Mathers looked at the binders on his desk that said, "Commandant Briefing," then looked back at Wilson.

"OK, Avery. But..."

"General, like always, sir, I will handle it."

☆

Ralph Pelham's office was spartan, like its inhabitant. The décor, absent any personal photos or mementos, told visitors very little about Pelham, and that's the way he liked it. As he sat behind his aircraft-carrier-sized desk, working on the computer and making notes, Terry Jamison and Charlie Thompson sat at a small conference table in the corner of the large office, at the opposite end of the cozy nook with the leather chairs. Terry fired off emails on his phone, Charlie studied the crossword book before him, and Pelham worked at his desk as if they weren't there. The library-like silence broke when Terry got a call on his cell phone.

"No, we're still waiting to meet—waste of goddamn time. Go ahead with the deposition. I won't be able to make it now."

There was a pause.

"No. Screw him."

Charlie looked up, annoyed that his concentration had been broken.

Terry scowled at Charlie but continued talking, "NO. We take it to trial. Anything else?"Another pause.

"OK. Talk to you later." He hung up, put the cell in the right breast pocket of his expensive, tailored gray pin-striped suit, and then adjusted his pink and grey silk tie.

Pelham looked at his watch and glanced at the two odd fellows at the conference table. A high-priced Black attorney had won a massive class action suit against the Bureau and an old field agent from Cleveland with about as much stature and ambition as a wrinkled suit. Pelham shook his head, pressed the intercom, and said, "Where the hell is Croft?"

Almost on cue, Inspector Nathaniel Croft entered, surveyed the situation, and said, "Gentlemen, sorry. Traffic. I see you've all had time to get well acquainted. This scene looks like Westside Story: Sharks on one side and jets on another."

Everyone looked at him with daggers. Nathaniel skipped the pleasantries, the long-time-no-see with Pelham. Nathaniel had never liked him because of what he had done to Terry and a host of other minorities who'd fallen under his boot. Suddenly, Nathaniel had a flashback and saw the face of his childhood buddy, Jerry Clapper. They'd been best friends for years until they went off to college, Nathaniel to Stanford and Jerry to Howard University. While Jerry was in DC his first year, he was shot and killed by a white police officer following a minor altercation at a Georgetown bar. The officer was never convicted despite a string of racial run-ins he'd had over the years—much like Ralph. And today, Nathaniel would intentionally let Ralph feel the weight of power on his neck.

"OK. Let's get down to business. Ralph, we'll need some things,'" Nathaniel said as he pulled a sheet of paper from his suit pocket. "I want secure office space. Need the files and evidence there by 2 PM today."

"Wait a second, Nate," Pelham said.

"It's Nathaniel, and you'll need to take some notes. There's a lot more."

Pelham paused a moment, then pressed the intercom again. "Watts, get in here and take notes." Pelham and Croft engaged in a staring contest for the thirty seconds it took Watts to appear. Now Nathaniel did feel like he was back in elementary school.

Once Watts was seated in an inconspicuous spot, her pen at the ready, Nathaniel continued down his to-do list with machine-gun delivery. "So, space, laptops, files, the autopsy report, lab results, a tech guy at our disposal, and all the forensics. We'll visit the crime scene after this meeting." Then, Nathaniel paused for dramatic effect. "Oh, and send all the agents detailed to work this case back to their offices. Rather than me reading the rest, I'll leave my list with you."

Nathaniel plunked down a yellow legal-sized sheet of paper with item after item in front of Pelham. Then he turned to Charlie and Terry. "Let's start with a tour of the crime scene, but first, I need to hit the head."

While Terry waited outside, Nathaniel and Charlie stood side-by-side at the urinals. Charlie turned to Nathaniel and spoke in a church whisper, "Are you outta your fuckin' mind, Sport? Jamison sued the crap out of the Bureau."

"That's exactly why I picked him."

"Huh?"

"A professor of mine at Stanford once told a class of aspiring writers, 'always keep your ardent critics closest.'"

"Speak English."

"Better to have Terry in the tent pissing out than out of the tent pissing in."

Nathaniel, Charlie, and Terry piled into a new black Ford Explorer driven by Jack Eller, Deputy Agent in Charge of the FBI Academy. Eller looked like a Marine who had just removed his uniform and put on a cheap suit. Sporting a buzz cut, he sat in the car like a sphinx. "Gentlemen, I'll escort you to the crime scene."

Nathaniel looked at him and said, "Oh, and I thought we were going to the Kennedy Center."

Charlie smiled, but Terry and Jack Eller sat stone-faced. Ten silent minutes later, they had parked and were crossing the area cordoned off by yellow police tape. Eller pointed to each critical landmark: "We think the victim was hit from the front somewhere over there, stripped, then dragged and cut over here. Strung up on this tree."

As Eller talked in the background, Nathaniel began to trek through the woods in ever-increasing concentric circles.

Terry listened too, watching Nathaniel walking in circles out of one eye. Charlie paid no attention to Nathaniel. By now, he was used to his unorthodox approach to investigations and everything else. About 50 yards beyond the yellow tape, Nathaniel stopped near a large old tree in a small clearing. He noticed pieces of bark had been peeled away. Nathaniel smelled the wood, looked at the crook of the tree branch just above his shoulder, and saw a broken toothpick. He pulled out an evidence bag and, with the edge of a pen, nudged some chips into it and the toothpick parts neatly into another. He gently kicked back some leaves, exposing footprints and scuff marks.

"I think they had a spotter over here—well beyond the crime scene. Some broken bark, a toothpick, and shuffle marks. It may be nothing, but it could be something. Let's get this to forensics to see if there's a relationship. Also, maybe take some pics of the tree and surrounding area."

Eller's face got bright red. "OK."

Then Nathaniel said, "Noon. Time for some of that fine Quantico haute cuisine. You can drop us at the canteen, can't you, Eller?" Nathaniel paid no attention whatsoever to Eller's black look.

7
THE LAUNCH

Tuesday, September 16

The executive conference room was located adjacent to Ralph Pelham's corner office. The large rectangular mahogany conference table seated 20 people comfortably—a number more during an emergency. The oak-paneled walls boasted the storied history of the Academy with plaques, awards, and framed patches from almost every police department in the US and friendly foreign departments. The American flag and the FBI's blue-and-gold flag stood in the corner. And on the wall behind the head of the table, the oversized FBI seal dominated the room.

Perched in front of the seal like royalty, Nathaniel sat at the head of the table with Charlie on one side of him and Terry on the other. They were all reading copies of the crime scene report on their confidential cells while waiting for their laptops and for Ralph to tell them which area of the Academy they would claim for the task force office. The remains of a working lunch still lingered on the table. The room was eerily quiet as the three men read intently. Occasionally there was the sound of a pen scratching as they each took notes.

The quiet was disturbed by a knock on the door, but before Nathaniel or any of the three could respond, Sergeant Major Avery Wilson entered, followed by a Marine Captain. Nathaniel remained seated and turned toward the two Marines. He glanced at the wiry Wilson, all taught and proper but quickly moved his gaze toward the captain, who had the most natural smile he'd ever seen. She wore the classic day uniform of drab green slacks and a beige short sleeve shirt. The Marine uniform does its best to obscure the female form, but in this instance, it failed. He had to look back at Wilson to keep his eyes from wandering further.

"Afternoon, sir. I'm Sergeant Major Avery T. Wilson, and this is Captain Samantha Melton." Both Marines extended their hands to shake with Nathaniel, who reached past Wilson to shake the captain's hand slowly and purposefully, then the sergeant's.

"My pleasure. What can I do for you?"

"To be blunt, sir, in eleven days, General Mathers, my boss, should be confirmed as the new Commandant of the Marine Corps."

"Congratulations to him and you. On September 25th, I believe, before the Senate."

"Exactly, Sir, and we'd like to keep things quiet 'til after his Senate confirmation."

"Good idea"

"Well, sir, the General was hopin' we could have Captain Melton here assigned to the taskforce—at least 'til the hearin's over."

Nathaniel smiled at the captain. Then turned to Sergeant Wilson and shook his head. "Sorry, but no."

Wilson's jaw tightened, then relaxed. "May I ask why, sir?"

"Just my style. Rest assured that we'll give the General a briefing if and when we turn up anything that might impact the Marine Corps. Now, if you'll excuse me, Sergeant Major and Captain, we must return to the case."

Wilson got a look in his eyes that could cut steel and said, "Excuse me, sir. But the Commandant has already spoken to Director Greenburg 'bout Captain Melton. Didn't you get the word yet? Here's the e-mail from the Director confirmin' it."

Wilson handed the email copy to Nathaniel, who read it and promptly returned it to him. He looked at Wilson and the Captain and said, "I'll get back to you on this, Sergeant. Nice to meet you, Captain."

Nathaniel sat down and re-engaged with the report as if the two Marines were gone.

The captain approached the door, but Wilson didn't move, "Sir, the General...."

Nathaniel took off his reading glasses and looked up at Wilson. "Sergeant, I said I would get back to you, and I will."

Wilson gritted his teeth, and a burst of anger flashed across his face, which he replaced quickly with a forced smile and nod that had been well practiced for years in the Marine Corps. "Yes, sir. We look forward to that."

"Son of a bitch!" spit out Sergeant Wilson once they were outside the Academy building. "Sorry 'bout that, Captain. You'll be on that task force, I promise you."

"No problem, Sergeant. Anything I can help with in your office? I'm not one to sit around," Sam said as they climbed into Wilson's Jeep.

"I'm sure there's something you can do, even if it's just figuring out where to put all the damn binders. Never in my life have I seen so many god-damn binders."

It was a hive of activity when they arrived at Wilson's office. A collection of cubicles held Marines working at computers. Wilson's office was a glass-walled room at the back, not far from a well-used coffee station. Along the left-hand side of the room, a copier was continuously in use, and a folding table along the back wall held an impressive array of briefing and background binders.

Before Wilson headed into his office, he said, "Get comfortable but not too comfortable...you won't be here long. I'll have you back on that FBI task force ASAP."

"So, you weren't kidding."

"No, I was not, Captain. I'll leave you with Captain Anton until we hear back from the damned FBI. Anton, Melton here is cooling her heels. Please put her to work."

"Will do." When Wilson had gone back to his office, Marge asked, "What was all that about?" Marge and Sam were neighbors on the women's floor of the bachelor officer's quarters, known as the BOQ, and had become fast friends.

"I went over to join the lynching task force, but some fancy-pants FBI suit told us politely to get lost. I thought Wilson was going to clock him one."

"I wouldn't put it past him. He gets tighter wound up daily, and there are still thirteen days until the hearings. By that point, he's going to be levitating from sheer adrenaline. Anyway, want to organize these deployment statistics into something intelligible? My assistant was supposed to do it, but I think he might have been buried under an avalanche of paper."

"I'm right here, ma'am," said a tall, long-suffering Samoan corporal as he stood up in the next cubicle.

"Jackson! There you are. Captain Melton is helping us out for a bit. Give her any of those stats sheets you have. And find her a chair."

"Yes, ma'am." He hurried off.

"Marge, are you torturing that poor corporal by pretending you can't see him when he's about seven feet tall?"

Marge grinned. "I told him if he impressed me, I'd put in a good word for him with the JAG corp. He's brilliant, and I think he'd make a fantastic JAG lawyer. But we could use a little humor around here lately."

Jackson returned with an office chair for Sam.

"Here you are, ma'am."

"Thanks, Jackson."

"Just pull up to my desk for now; not a free one anywhere. You doing anything later?"

"No, why?"

"Want to get a drink? We start prep tomorrow with the general, and I've been cast as Hostile Senator. I want one night of downtime before things get crazy."

"You're quizzing the general?"

"I am, indeed. That's why they brought me down from D.C. I've got the trial experience to play a bad guy. Ensure the general doesn't have an A-Few-Good-Men moment before Congress."

"You know, he does look a little like Jack Nicholson…"

Marge laughed. "I won't tell him you said that."

When you enter the Office of the FBI Director on the 7th floor of the J. Edgar Hoover Building at 10th and Pennsylvania Avenue in the District of Columbia, better known as Mahogany Row, you arrive in a waiting room about the size of a pickleball court. Adjoining the waiting room is the office occupied by the Director's security detail supervisory agent. Near the entrance, a uniformed guard is positioned to check in all escorted guests—who'd already been through a vetting process at the building's security center just off 10th Street. Then you waited for entry into the next room, where the Director's Executive Assistants worked. Once several secreted cameras thoroughly filmed you at different angles, the guard would buzz you into their domain—also surveilled for security. They would then escort guests into a cavernous conference room with a massive oblong table, able to sit up to 30 people and 40 in a pinch.

Then, if you were privileged to be invited into the holy of holies—the Director's inner "chambers"—you'd notice that the air was different. Here "chambers" were formal but personal, with seascape artwork on the walls and an array of family photos on the credenza behind the Director's massive judge's chair that could have passed for a costly leather Barcalounger. A former federal appeals court judge, Ann Greenburg considered her "chambers" where the critical and often informal, sometimes contentious, but always honest, conversation was allowed outside her massive conference room, her FBI version of a courtroom.

Two leather wing chairs, formal but comfortable, sat in front of her massive, pristine desk. At the opposite end of the room from the director's desk, which overlooked Pennsylvania Avenue, was an informal conversation nook with another leather wing chair facing a leather couch. If you were a friend or family of the Director or a dignitary of sufficient status, upon your entry, the Director would come out from behind her desk—a signal for the escort to guide you to the couch.

And with the grace and charm of a Vogue model turned diplomat, she would walk up to the visiting dignitary and warmly shake their hand as if they were old friends. Her charm and gracious smile were disarming and immediately set the tone for friendly, open conversation. The Director was attractive and athletic with streaked blond hair, piercing hazel eyes, trim and fit. In heels, the former Princeton volleyball player, the Director, was at eye level with even the tallest men and women.

However, she stayed seated behind her desk for this meeting and repeated what she'd already told him once. "Nathaniel, I've told you that this is political. I also told you that I promised the Commandant absolute cooperation, including a single representative on the task force. It's just one person, and I've given you free rein on everything else," she said with a look that said, "and don't make me regret it."

Sitting in one of the two large wing chairs in front of the Director's desk, Nathaniel leaned forward to argue his case. "All due respect, Director, this may come back to bite us. We risk confidentiality issues and gain nothing. What's more—"

She deliberately hit the desk with her hand as if it were a gavel.

"Nathaniel, it's a done deal. Period. You know how politics work. The deputy commandant has a real bee in his bonnet about his upcoming confirmation hearings, and he wants this dealt with ASAP."

He glared back at her, then quickly erased any hint of anger as he recognized her steel-piercing eyes leveled at his. No blinking there. Besides, he smelled the hint of Chanel No. 5, which his mother had worn.

"Yes, Director. I just..."

"Of course, I also want this dealt with as quickly as possible. But I want to see justice done and the culprit punished. I could give a damn about his Senate hearing. But things will go smoother if he thinks I'm on his side. Do I make myself clear?" she said, standing up in full array like an eagle about to attack lesser prey. She walked with purpose from behind her desk toward the door leading to the conference room with Nathaniel in tow. Terry and Charlie stood up when the Director and Nathaniel entered, but she waved them back into their seats.

"Charlie, good to see you, and Terry, great to see you on our side of the courtroom this time."

He smiled. "Thank you, Director."

"OK. Let's get started," she said, looking at Nathaniel, still licking his wounds.

Nathaniel sat taller and said, "We're sifting through the initial interviews and forensics. We've got the CaseMaster system crunching the data from all the initial interviews for analysis, linkages, and leads. We'll reinterview anyone who we think is relevant. We've sent evidence to the CODIS lab guys for DNA analysis. We have unlimited access to investigators from the Washington Field Office; however, I'm keeping it a tight circle until we determine the next steps."

Nathaniel turned toward Charlie and gestured to him to chime in. Charlie cleared his throat and said, "The victim is

Mohammed Rasheed, formerly known as Stanley Whitcomb, a detective from the Detroit Police Department. A former Marine, Whitcomb fought in Afghanistan, worked in a Ford plant, took up Islam, changed his name to Mohammed Rasheed, and started night school at Wayne State. He met a Detroit cop who got him interested in becoming a police officer. He had a meteoric rise in the department due to his undercover work. He got an early recommendation to the National Academy. Not the friendliest guy who ever lived, according to some early interviews at the academy, but not one to intentionally pick a fight or back away from one. "

"What about family?" asked the Director.

Nathaniel responded, "I'm flying out to interview his ex-wife and grown son later today. Rasheed has been divorced for years. No current partner, as far as we can tell."

"Tell me about the forensics," said the Director.

"Rasheed was killed by blunt force trauma to the right side of the head. According to the coroner and forensics, the blow was probably delivered by a pipe or an aluminum bat."

Charlie pointed first to the autopsy and then to the crime scene photos. "Looks like three attackers—based on shoe castings—two big guys about the same size, and a third guy of medium height, estimated by shoe sizes of 12 and 9, respectively. Footprints were consistent with NA and new agent footgear purchased or distributed through the PX. The body was found swinging from a tree by an agent running in the woods maybe an hour after the murder. No other witnesses. Trace fibers under the victim's fingernails match fibers from NA T-shirts."

He pointed this out in a photo showing the victim's fingernails before removing the substance. Then he offered another side-by-side comparison of green fiber from the victim's fingernails and fiber from a sample standard NA polo shirt—a precise match.

The Director interrupted, "Are you implying it was another National Academy student?"

Charlie cleared his throat and said, "Fiber comparisons and shoe treads point to an NA student. But that could all be a smokescreen. Plenty of visitors buy shirts and shoes at the Academy PX. But we are tracking down the PX records to see if there were any odd purchases of shoes of different sizes or three polo shirts together in a single purchase. We're not expecting a lot because there are many bulk purchases with each new NA class, which was only a few weeks before the murder. Anyway, the coroner fixed the time of death somewhere between 5 and 6 AM—the same with mutilation. The victim was mutilated postmortem—not much blood. He had a 5-by-5-centimeter swastika carved on his left pectoral. Also, maybe a smokescreen—I don't know yet. No weapon found."

"Any more about the victim?" asked the Director.

Nathaniel injected, "By several accounts, Rasheed was prickly. According to some folks interviewed before we arrived, he had a bit of a chip on his shoulder."

"White NA students, probably," said Terry.

Nathaniel said, "Director, we have a report that we can leave with you. Pretty detailed. But the bottom line is that we don't have any suspects yet."

That's when Terry said, "Actually, we may have a lead."

Nathaniel and Charlie looked at Terry with a say-what look on both faces.

"Yesterday, I was stopped by a Black NA student from Detroit. Wants to meet me tonight."

The Director closed her notebook. "OK. So, we have some progress to report to the Attorney General, whose office has called several times daily. Good. Let me know directly if anything comes of that meeting, Terry."

"Yes, Terry, we'll ALL be anxious to know," Nathaniel said as he looked at Charlie.

The Director's aide stood at the doorway and signaled to her by pointing to his watch.

The Director nodded to the aide, stood up, and said, "OK, gentlemen. Leave the report with me. The Attorney General has called a mandatory meeting. Oh, one last thing. I've already told Nathaniel that I have promised the Commandant I'd allow the Marines to have an officer on the task force. It's political. No discussion, "the Director said as she looked at Nathaniel. Then she headed for the doorway, where two sizeable plain-clothes security guards joined her and escorted her out.

8
TOUR GUIDE

Wednesday, September 17

Two factors ensured the task force got prime space in the Washington building at the Academy, which also included a dormitory to accommodate late-night work. The first happened fortuitously when the behavioral sciences unit decided to move to a much larger space in the third sub-basement of the Academy. More secure, much larger, and more mystical, it matched the team of psychologists and behavioral scientists' personalities. The second was the more powerful of the two: Nathaniel's close and oddly contentious relationship with the Director. Some speculated that it was a battle of the bluebloods.

Nonetheless, she often accommodated his needs—usually to suit her own. In this case, as quick a resolution as possible. Prime space was a small price.

The space had been initially a TV lounge for National Academy students. But as the Academy got pushed to take on more responsibilities and personnel, some of the social spaces were converted into workplaces. The eight substantial interior glass windows overlooked the Academy courtyard: a large expanse between the original two dorms that housed about 1,000 students. A couple of monuments adorned the ample open space, along with new brickwork, and chairs and tables had been added to make it look more hospitable, but to no avail. It still felt like no man's land.

The task force office was comprised of seven cubicles, one

private office, and a small storage room. Nathaniel liked how small it was; that meant it would be hard to add many new people without moving. On Wednesday morning, Charlie, seated outside Nathaniel's office in the first cubicle, was engrossed in reading through a stack of reports. Terry was on the phone toward the back of the office—almost on another planet.

At precisely 9 AM, dressed in her summer service uniform—a tapered, cutaway tan short-sleeved blouse sporting two rows of ribbons, expert marksmanship badges, and matching trousers—Captain Samantha "Sam" Melton stood tall and ready for work. On her collar sat captain's bars, often referred to as railroad tracks because that's exactly what they looked like. She was tall, lean, and athletic, with raven black hair in a tight bun and make-up-free hazel green eyes. Being both good-looking and female in a male-dominated job, Sam had to work twice as hard to prove herself. She knew the FBI agents she was about to work with would view her with distrust.

She squared her shoulders and hit the doorframe a couple of times. "Hello?" she said, first tentatively and then more forcefully. "Is anyone home?" She saw Charlie, head down in his cubicle, and walked toward him until she stood right in front of the opening to his cubicle. She cleared her throat, waited, then said, "Hello, sir." Nothing. Then she banged on the side of the cubicle and bellowed, "HELLO, sir."

Charlie felt the vibration and heard a muffled voice. Sam's presence startled him, and he knocked over his coffee. "Shit, I mean, hello, Captain. I'm sorry, I'm a klutz—" he said, mopping up the last few swallows of lukewarm coffee.

Sam smiled and said, "I'm sorry if I startled you, sir."

"Truth is, my hearing aids were turned down, and please call me Charlie."

She laughed, thinking he was kidding until he adjusted them as they spoke. She quickly wiped away the smile.

"That's OK. I'm not exactly the TV version of an FBI agent."

"You look fine to me, Charlie," she said, extending her hand.

Charlie smiled and shook her hand. "Thanks, Sport, but my James Bond days are behind me. It turns out it screws up your hearing when you're feet away from an explosion. It's not as exciting as it sounds. Well, I'll give you the grand tour. Over here, we have a desk ready for you."

At about the same time, Terry wandered up to the front of the office. He pointed to an empty cubicle and said, "Hi, I'm Terry Jamison. I'm the third wheel of the group."

"Hey, Terry, I'm Sam. I guess that makes me the fourth wheel."

"I'll leave you in Charlie's capable hands," said Terry as he returned to his cube by the window. "Oh, and I hope you don't like coffee. What's in the pot over there barely qualifies."

Sam laughed, and Charlie said, "I bet you're used to the government sludge. We can't all have an espresso machine in our fancy downtown office." If Terry heard, he didn't dignify the comment with a reply.

Charlie spread his arms. "So, this is the office. Any questions?"

"I like what you've done with the place, Charlie."

He looked at the stack of reports on his desk and smiled back at her. "Yeah, I call it post-modern stacking."

She laughed.

"You want something to drink? I think we've got some soda, along with the sludge."

"Just some water."

Charlie grabbed a paper cup, filled it at the bubbler, and handed it to Sam, who took a sip and looked around.

"Is Inspector Croft here now?"

"No, Nate, er, Nathaniel's in Detroit conducting some interviews."

"Good old reliable Nathan, Nathan, Nathan Detroit," she sang. Charlie looked blank, but she heard Terry's deep laugh from his desk. "Glad there's at least one musical theatre fan here."

"I used to be his training officer 20 years ago. Now he's Croft, Nathaniel Croft," said Charlie, affecting a bad English accent.

Sam laughed.

"Look, Sam, I know this has to be a little, ah, strange."

She nodded.

"Nathaniel's a good guy."

She looked straight at Charlie and said, "Yeah, I'm sure he rescues kittens from trees and knits hats for orphans in his spare time."

"Hah! The idea of Nathaniel sitting still long enough to knit anything… he's got a lot of skills, but I'm pretty sure needlework isn't one of them."

They lapsed into silence.

"Well, listen. The boss didn't leave instructions for what he wanted you to work on, and I've only got one crossword book. You ever been to the Academy before?"

"No, never."

"You want a quick tour? Give you a feel for the place. What do you say?"

"Sounds like a plan to me. Always been curious about this place."

"Well then." He opened the door with an exaggerated bow. "Madame, if you please?"

Charlie put on his best tour-guide face. "We'll start with the gerbil tubes."

"The… what?"

"You'll see," said Charlie as he hit the up arrow to summon the elevator. Up on the dorm floor, they came to a glass tunnel that led to the classroom building, making it possible to walk from one to the other in the winter, even in short sleeves.

They walked past the faculty offices and various departments, like leadership, communications, and legal. "Offices. You have seen one; you seen 'em all. But the classrooms are pretty cool." He led the way to the second floor. "The classrooms were designed in the early '70s, but you'd never know it because of regular technical upgrades."

"Wow." Sam took in the tiered classroom that could hold up to 50 people, with swivel chairs and rear screen projection. "There's enough tech in here to launch a satellite."

"Yeah, the Bureau never met a gadget it didn't love. Ok, let's go see some of the fun stuff."

He took her to the gym, where they saw new agents on the mats wrestling each other down and putting on handcuffs. Most of them had just left corporate America, grad school, or law school, and so needed to develop the street smarts and physical strength they'd need to survive in the field—all except for the ex-cops. There were always a few in every class; you could pick them out immediately during these exercises.

Next, they toured the pool. Sam noticed the green army fatigue pants and shirts hanging on the wall.

"So, what's that all about?" she asked, pointing to the laundry display.

"Agents and SWAT teams practice what affectionately is known as 'drown proofing' or doing whatever it takes to stay afloat. They put on the clothes, jump into the pool, learn how to shed them, scoop up the air, and use them as flotation devices."

"Yep, it reminds me of the Naval Academy, but we had to wear our own clothes!"

"So, you went to Annapolis—impressive."

"I guess so, but I got in on athletics, not my scholastic skills."

"What's your sport?"

"Soccer."

"Did you play at the Academy?"

"Sure did, until I tore my ACL."

"Ouch."

"You bet. But I'm back to running five miles a day with no pain, so all's well."

"Let me show you the running trails and the Yellow Brick Road."

"Sounds cool—maybe see Dorothy, the Tin Man, the Lion, and the Scarecrow too?"

Charlie smiled. "I have a lot of sympathy for the Tin Man these days."

They exited the gym's back door and walked toward a tree at the entrance to a path. On the tree were several signs, among them "Hurt," "Agony," "Pain," and "Love It!"

Charlie walked with Sam toward the start of the Yellow Brick Road, a grueling rite of passage for NA students. It was a 10K cross-country torture chamber through hills, woods, walls to be scaled, climbing ropes, barbed wire, water to be navigated, and much more to challenge even the fittest athlete. The road was the final fitness test for NA students, and all who passed were presented with their own personal Yellow Brick with their NA class number on it.

"If you're ever in a police station and see a yellow brick, you'll know why."

"Wait, you get a yellow brick if you finish? That's much cooler than a badge or a certificate. I can't wait to give it a go. If that's OK with you and the Inspector."

"As long as I don't have to do it with you, I say have at it! I'm an old man now. My Yellow Brick Road days are behind me."

"But you ran it once upon a time, right?"

"I'm afraid that information is classified, ma'am," said Charlie with a wink. "But if you think that's cool, wait till you see Hogan's Alley."

A short distance away, they came to a large sign:

WELCOME TO HOGAN'S ALLEY.

CAUTION: Law enforcement training exercise in progress.

Display of weapons, the firing of blank ammunition, and arrests may occur. If challenged, please follow the instructions.

Ironically as a State Trooper handing you a speeding ticket, the sign ended with: HAVE A NICE DAY.

"What's this? Is that a laundromat, I see?"

"The town with the highest crime rate in America. Hollywood set designers built it to help with new agent training. Looks real, doesn't it?"

"It's almost spooky."

"Actors roam the mean streets of Hogan, impersonating mobsters, terrorists, muggers, and drug dealers. It looks like any town in America, except the bank gets robbed at least twice a week, and the motel has seen more drug busts than even the seediest motel in Vegas."

"Are these all real buildings, or are some just facades?"

"A lot of them are real. But if you try to see what's playing at the Biograph movie theater, you'll find it's just a front for FBI field training rooms."

"This is so cool! Do students ever just come to hang out to watch the action?"

"I think they're all trying to be too cool for that, but the tourists sure do. Hey, you want a coffee?" Charlie gestured to The Dogwood Inn Restaurant across the street.

"I wouldn't say no. So, this is a real restaurant?" Sam asked as they crossed the street. Before Charlie could answer, they both turned at the sound of a car speeding down the main road, hotly pursued by two cars full of new agents. The agent cars performed a near-perfect blocking maneuver, pulled over the would-be bank robbers, yanked them out of the vehicle, and cuffed them.

"Ok, Charlie, did you plan that?"

Charlie laughed. "I wish I could take credit, but alas. Course, if you hang out on Main Street for any length of time, you're bound to see something like that."

"Think we'll get held up while we're having coffee?" asked Sam as Charlie held the door for her. "I've never been held up before!

Of course, I've never been excited by the prospect until now."

The Dogwood was a classic American diner, all chrome and Formica and that specific shade of pistachio green. The servers wore pink and blue uniforms, and the menus were a pale butter yellow. They sat on stools at the counter. "Wow, this whole place is done in the shade of dinner mint, huh?" said Sam, and Charlie laughed. A middle-aged waitress with short curly hair and a nametag that said Doris approached them.

"What'll ya have, hun?" she asked, pencil poised over her order pad. "A large coffee with cream and sugar to go, please," said Charlie.

Doris turned her gaze to Sam. "Large coffee with whole milk to go, please." Doris bustled away and returned a minute later with the coffees. Charlie put a five on the counter. "Thanks, Doris." She nodded and scooped up the bill. They headed for the door.

Sam took a sip of coffee. "Is this the cheapest coffee on the entire East Coast? It's good too."

"I think they charge the tourists more. But it beats the heck out of the sludge in the office."

"So, what's next?"

"Well, let's see. You want to see the firearms ranges? Also, how about the Hostage Rescue Team's shooting house?"

"That sounds great. I don't suppose the profilers are on the tour?"

"Nah, they're tucked away in a basement somewhere. Bunch of weirdos." Sam laughed.

They ended up at the PX, stocked with the always popular FBI T-shirts, sweatshirts, hats, and memorabilia.

"Can I interest you in a t-shirt?"

"No thanks, I have plenty, thanks to the Corps." They strolled on.

"Here's the cafeteria. Want to grab some lunch before we head back?"

"Great plan. I'm starved."

Charlie headed straight for his usual turkey sandwich, but Sam took a full lap, taking in all the offerings. She found Charlie at a table by a sunny window.

"I was overwhelmed by choice! But the stir-fry looked too good to pass up. What'd you get?"

"Turkey and cheese on whole wheat, side salad, and chips. If I'm feeling fancy, I ask them to toast the bread. But this is my standard lunch. Can't teach an old dog new tricks."

"You can't be that old, grandpa, if the FBI will still have you. Don't you guys have a mandatory retirement age?"

"That's true. About 11 months before I clock out and put my feet up. I feel old. My wife died last year, which knocked the wind out of my sails."

"I'm so sorry to hear that, Charlie," Sam said with genuine empathy.

"But you don't want to hear an old man complain. What'd you think of the tour?"

"It was great! That's the most fun I've had in a long while."

"Thanks, but I'm not sure if I should feel good or bad for you if that's the highlight of your social life! Maybe I'm not the only one who needs to get out more."

"Touché. I'm just back from a war zone, so civilian life is still exciting."

"If you don't mind me saying so, Sport, it must be hard to be a beautiful woman in a field full of men."

"That's perceptive of you, Charlie."

"Not particularly. I've seen many heads turn today, and once I double-checked, I remembered to put on pants this morning. That only leaves you."

"It's true. I think the command structure helps, but I'm not sure it does. But I'll tell you one rule I've always stuck to—I don't date Marines."

"Sensible. My training officer used to say, 'don't shit where you eat,' if you'll pardon the expression."

Sam laughed. "That's for sure."

"Sam, I've got a question for you."

"Sure."

"Why you? How'd you get picked for this assignment?"

"I'm new, just checked in—back from Afghanistan and a special intel assignment. Also, I've yet to be assigned at Quantico, and I guess I fit the stereotype that Sergeant Wilson was looking for: Someone who might not ruffle feathers but know enough to get him the intel feedback he wanted for the General. I'm also NCIS, so there's a plausible reason to have me here."

Charlie looked thoughtful. "Well, Sam, I appreciate your candor."

"Listen, I'm a Marine first, but what I'm not is a spy. Unlike the rest of you, I suppose," she said with a smile. "I obey orders but don't like being sent on a mission without all the intel. And I don't care for being used as a means to an end."

"I get that for sure. You know Nathaniel transferred me here for the task force without asking me first?" Sam's eyebrows went up. "You'll be the direct liaison to the Marine Corps. Any contact with the Marines will come and go through you. Only one rule: what happens in the task force stays in the task force. Only people with a need to know get told anything we do."

Sam nodded. "Absolutely. One last question."

"Shoot."

"I spy a coffee bar in the corner there. Should we bring a coffee back for Terry?"

"I'm tempted to say Fancypants can get his own, but you're a better person than I am. Lead the way."

9
THE INVESTIGATION BEGINS

Wednesday, September 17

After a 40-minute Uber ride from the airport, Nathaniel arrived at the Whitcomb home in the upscale Detroit suburb of Birmingham. Located 20 miles north of Detroit, Birmingham was an upper-middle-class community of only 4 square miles and nearly 20,000 residents—only 1% of whom were African American—including the Whitcomb family. Rasheed had insisted that his family live there despite the demographics. The schools were great, the town was safe, and the people sophisticated—like he and his wife, Shari, an attorney at a prestigious Detroit law firm.

Nathaniel knocked on the front door of the white-with-black-shutters colonial, which Shari Whitcomb answered. She was tall and slender, in her late 50s, with light skin and subtle streaks of white in her black hair.

"Good afternoon, Mrs. Whitcomb. I'm Nathaniel Croft with the FBI. We spoke on the phone yesterday," he said, offering his credentials.

She looked at them briefly and said, "Please come in."

She led him into the living room. Sparse but elegant, the room's focal point was a large oriental rug framed by two overstuffed leather chairs and a leather couch draped with a throw blanket that matched the carpet. On the sofa sat Shari's son, Randal. In his late 20s, tall, trim, and muscular, wearing a University of Michigan blue-and-maize sweatshirt, he stood up and adjusted his horned-rimmed glasses as Nathaniel entered the living room.

"Agent Croft, this is my son, Randal."

Randal nodded and cautiously stuck out his hand to shake Nathaniel's outstretched one.

"Go, Wolverines," said Nathaniel pointing at the gold M on Randal's shirt.

Randal gave a quick smile and then sat back down on the couch.

"Thanks for agreeing to talk to me. Of course. I bring the Director's deepest condolences at the loss of your ex-husband, Mrs. Whitcomb, and your father, Randal. And I can assure you that whoever did this heinous act will be tracked down and prosecuted to the fullest extent of the law."

She nodded slightly and sat on the couch next to Randal. She gestured towards one of the leather club chairs, and Nathaniel sat down. He pulled out his iPhone and set it on the coffee table. "Mrs. Whitcomb, do you mind if I record our conversation? I prefer to give you my full attention rather than trying to scribble notes."

"I don't mind. Randal?" He shook his head.

"Thank you," said Nathaniel, hitting "record" on a voice memo. "What can you tell me about your ex-husband? What kind of guy was he?"

She thought for a moment or two and then said slowly and deliberately, "Complex."

"How so?

"After tours in Iraq and Afghanistan, he changed. He became angrier, more militant about the racial disparity he witnessed in the Marine Corps."

Nathaniel asked, "What did that racial disparity look like to him?"

"More dangerous assignments went to African Americans. When it came to discipline, they got more severe sentences. Not unlike what you see today in too many places in America, Inspector Croft."

"Regrettably so, Mrs. Whitcomb."

"Eventually, he converted to Islam and changed his name to Mohammed Rasheed," she said in a tone that turned flintier, harsher. "Randal and I remain Methodists."

"So, he converted to Islam after returning from Afghanistan?"

"Yes, twenty years ago, but he was introduced to it in-country. Several Black soldiers had gotten interested in the faith while in Iraq and Afghanistan. When he came home, Stanley got his job back at the car factory in Hamtramck—an assembly plant in a rough neighborhood."

"Hamtramck, isn't that now GM's all-electric car plant?"

"Yes, it happened in 2021. They were going to close it but decided to rebrand it—an autonomous vehicle plant."

"Please continue, Mrs. Whitcomb."

"When he worked there, Stanley got hooked up with other Black Muslims, many vets. Then, we had Randal," she said as she looked over and smiled at her son. "That's when Stanley decided to return to school at night to get his degree. It only took him three years because they credited him for his military training."

"I'm sorry to ask this, but did his conversion strain your marriage?"

"Of course it did, Inspector. But after all, we'd been through with his deployment, law school, and getting our lives set up, he was still the man I married. The change would come later."

"Where'd he go to school?"

"Wayne State. He took criminal justice—wanted to change things. He met a Black Detroit police officer who taught as an adjunct in the Criminal Justice program. They became friends. Eventually, Stanley left GM and became a Detroit police officer. That's when we moved to Birmingham from Detroit. Stanley wanted Randal to get the best education possible and for us to live in a safe town."

"How'd that move go?"

"Not well. Birmingham is as white as small towns get. We struggled. Stanley and I fought—a lot. I was finishing law school at night, also at Wayne State, Randal was bullied at school, and Stanley worked undercover narcotics. Things were unhealthy. Finally, Stanley walked out. He's been an angry man since returning from Afghanistan, but when he left," she hesitated to catch herself and said, "A good man doesn't leave when things get tough, Inspector."

"Yes, ma'am, I believe that. He ever tell you what happened in Afghanistan?"

"No. The harder I tried, the more he withdrew."

"After he left, did he stay in contact?"

"He came back for a few of Randal's birthdays. He always sent him a card and some money. After I got established in my law practice, I started sending back his checks until they eventually stopped," she said. "Parenting is a lot more than a check once a year. And as much as Stanley wanted to change the world, he left his son, his only child, basically fatherless. Change starts at home."

"Anyone have any reason to hurt him?"

"I'm not the best person to ask about that. But he was pretty vocal when it came to racism. He was also adamant about Islam, and some other cops resented that."

"Like who?"

"I don't know anyone in particular. Stanley complained about people I didn't know, and I kept his work at arm's length from our family."

Nathaniel turned toward Randal. "Randal, can you remember anyone who might have had a score to settle with your father?"

Randal laughed. "Other than me? Look, my father deserted my mother and me when I was just a kid. Just walked away. He insisted on moving here, and then he left." He reached over and slid his hand over his mother's.

"I understand. Anything about him, his buddies, anyone who can help us?"

Randal paused and looked down. "Not really."

Nathaniel studied Randal carefully and said, "I think you might."

Shari looked at her son and nodded. "Tell him about the letter."

Randal took off his glasses, rubbed his eyes, and spoke slowly. "After Dad left, maybe a year ago, he sent me a letter."

Randal stood up, moved toward a bookcase brimming with books, and pulled out a weathered King James Bible. He extracted a letter and opened it carefully.

He began to read. "I know I've not been a good father to you. When I returned from my tour in Afghanistan, something inside me had died. I lost faith in everything, including the Marine Corps. My platoon sergeant and lieutenant put Black Marines on patrol point like throwaways—especially proud, outspoken ones. I lost three brothers that way. When I returned to the States, I sent letters to the Commandant of the Marine Corps, my Congressman, and even a Senator. All I got back were form letters thanking me for my concern—no action, nothing. The system will never change. Don't trust a white man."

Randal paused, a catch in his voice.

"I love you, son. Take care of your mother; she's a great woman."

Shari also began to cry as she reached over to grab Randal's hand and held it tightly. Silence filled the room as Randal collected himself and slowly refolded the letter to return it to the bible.

Nathaniel sat quietly to show his respect. "Randal, may I take a photo of that letter?" Randal nodded and retrieved the letter. As he carefully opened the letter, Nathaniel noticed it had been stored between the Old and New Testaments.

☆

That evening just before 7 pm, Terry entered the first floor of the Academy library—a large open area with reference books, periodicals, and a massive checkout desk with a half-asleep librarian. By this time in the evening, the head research librarian's office, just off the open area, had been vacated. Over the checkout desk, a large open atrium was in the middle of the library. Terry looked up the three stories toward the recessed ceiling and climbed up the stairs to the law library on the third floor.

As he ascended, he passed periodicals and books particular to the Academy —journals like *The Forensic Science Journal*, *The FBI Law Enforcement Bulletin*, and books like *Murder Investigation* and *Understanding the Serial Rapist.*

When he finally got to the third floor, it looked like any extensive law office library with the US Code lining the shelves. At one of the tables near the back of the room sat Isaac Welty, a Black National Academy student wearing a typical NA outfit: a green polo shirt with the NA logo, khaki pants, and black leather athletic shoes. His height was not apparent until he stood to shake Terry's hand.

"Terry?" Isaac queried as he extended his right hand that quickly enveloped Terry's.

"Hi, Isaac. Terry Jamison," Terry said as he shook hands and then took a seat. "I got your email. You showed quite the initiative in getting in touch. How'd you know where to find me?"

"I saw you speak at the last National Organization of Black Law Enforcement Executives about your class-action suit against the Bureau. It made an impression since I'd already applied to the NA by then."

"Never thought I'd be back inside the FBI, but here I am. You wanted to talk to me about Mohammed?"

Isaac looked around quickly, then spoke in a calm voice. "I used to study here with Mohammed. Smart guy."

"Were you in the same classes?"

"We were in a leadership class working group."

"What was he like?"

"Mohammed is—was—an in-your-face kinda guy."

"Not Mr. Congeniality?"

Isaac smiled and shook his head.

"You know of anyone who might have wanted to hurt him?"

Isaac looked away and said, "Not really."

"You sure about that?" Terry leaned in closer.

Isaac leaned back. He looked around.

"Hard to say."

"Give it a try."

"OK. Two guys in our section. Weightlifters. Keep to themselves. Eat, study, and work out together."

"Names?"

Isaac seemed to be weighing what he was about to say. Terry didn't rush him. Finally, in a low voice, he said, "Alex Roland. Um, he's from Detroit Sheriff's Department. The other guy is Hershel Jones from the Louisiana State Police."

Terry wrote down the two names in a small black notebook.

"Why them?"

Again, Isaac looked around before he continued. "The morning Mohammed was killed, I saw Alex come back very early from the gym, which was unusual for him. I was on my way over to eat. I always take the stairs for exercise. Saw Alex bounding up them. Didn't say a word."

"And that struck you as odd?"

"Hershel wasn't in sight, and those two were joined at the hip. Plus, Alex was dressed all in black and looked like he'd already had a workout. I'm sure it doesn't seem like much to you, but one thing they teach you here is to look for patterns. This was not his pattern."

"Point taken. The FBI does love a pattern; I remember that from my time here. What else can you tell me about Alex and Hershel?"

"Not much. Stick to themselves. Except that Alex had a round tattoo removed from his bicep. You might want to check that out."

"Why? Lots of guys have tattoos taken off."

"Yeah, especially white supremacists coming to the FBI Academy."

"Oh shit, of course! Isaac, thanks for talking to me. If you think of anything else, let me know. And put the word out: I want to talk to anybody who might have seen or heard something. I'm not a company man, and my email is always open." Terry shook Isaac's hand and set off briskly down the stairs.

10
TWISTS AND TURNS

Thursday, September 18

About eight the following morning, Nathaniel was driving down 95 South in Virginia, listening to a classical music station and thinking about his whirlwind trip to Detroit. He liked classical music for letting his brain percolate: plenty of movement to keep the mind active, no words to distract, and the pieces were long, so there were fewer interruptions. He'd hoped to make it to the office yesterday but got in at 9 pm last night. As he cruised down the off-ramp, he pulled over to put down the hard top of his BMW. He loved the wind in his face, and he always marveled at the German engineering that folded a hardtop into three equal parts and tucked it neatly into the trunk. Those Germans, he thought.

As he approached the Marine guards, he stopped to show them his ID and let them savor his pearl-white James Bond ride.

"Thank you, sir. Have a good day. Sweet ride, sir," said the lance corporal with awe and longing in his voice.

Nathaniel gave a civilian salute and nod to the sentry and moved out quickly, navigating the 5 miles of tree-lined road that led to the FBI Academy.

When Nathaniel walked into the task force office, he saw Sam sitting beside Charlie. And when Charlie spotted him, he bolted up to intercept Nathaniel, pulled him into Nathaniel's office, and closed the door.

"Listen, Sport. She's a good kid. Smart. Naval Academy, the Expeditionary War School, NCIS. I spent most of the day with her yesterday. No bullshit. Give her a chance."

"Not like I have a choice."

"Yeah, but don't go out of your way to make it tough for her. I think she's much more an asset than a liability. She was honest with me about why she was here. Knows it's because Wilson wants a spy on the inside."

Nathaniel paused as he thought over his old mentor's suggestion. Then he nodded, OK.

Charlie smiled and came back a moment later with Sam.

"Sir, Captain Samantha Melton reporting as ordered." She stood straight-backed in front of his desk.

"Listen, Captain, let's clear the air. I've got nothing against the Marine Corps or you. It's a trust thing with me. My issue, not yours."

"Sir, first, it's Sam. Second, I respect your concern for trust. This is an uneasy situation. One might even say FUBAR."

Nathaniel laughed and said, "F'd Up Beyond Repair! Touché, Sam, and let's drop the sir thing."

"Yes, sir. I mean inspector."

"How about Nathaniel?"

"Happy to be on the team, uh, Nathaniel."

There was a long pause.

"Do I have to say 'dismissed'?" asked Nathaniel with a grin.

Sam looked momentarily embarrassed, then smiled. "It's the only sure way to get rid of a jarhead." She headed back to her desk, smiling to herself.

But as she passed Charlie's, he stared at his desk like he'd never seen it before.

"It's just a laptop, Charlie. It won't bite," joked Sam.

"Hmm? Oh, very funny. It's not the laptop, but there is something wrong. I, uh, I leave my desk a certain way every night. I set alarms."

Nathaniel had come out of his office searching for coffee and overheard Charlie's last comment. "For God's sake, Charlie. Are you still doing that paranoid stuff?"

Charlie nodded. Still distracted, he felt under his desk drawer.

He looked up at Nathaniel and said smugly, "Well, it ain't paranoia if they're really out to get you! The piece of tape under my desk drawer is broken." He looked over at his dictionary.

"Hmm. I always leave my dictionary on my work papers pointed due North.

But now it's pointing more East. Someone was in this office last night. After 7, when I left."

By now, Terry had come over as well.

"No one but us has access. Even the cleanup crew is escorted. Anyone else on our team come by after Charlie closed up shop?"

Sam said, "I don't even have a key yet."

"I met Welty at 7 pm and then went home," Terry said.

"Let me install a small fish-eye camera that'll record anyone who enters the office after hours. I can do it tonight, " Charlie said. "We had a similar case in Cleveland when a night clerk stole and sold supplies online. Dumb, but true."

"OK," Nathaniel said, quickly adding, "But no sound, or we need a court order. Go ahead with the digital camera. And everyone, lock your desks. We'll lock it in the safe every night if anything is hypersensitive. And since we're all here, let's have our first meeting." He pulled up a desk chair and motioned for the others to do the same.

"Well, welcome to the circus, everyone. This is a high-profile crime, and it happened in the Bureau's backyard. We are pressured to wrap this thing up as fast as possible. The thing is, I don't give a damn about timelines. What I care about is finding out who did this and why. The Director put me on this personally, and she knows what I'm like." Charlie snorted. "I wouldn't have brought Terry back if I'd wanted a team of yes men. I want a team of crack investigators, and that's what I have. Everything we do here is need-to-know. If you get pushback, I'm happy to play bad cop. We're a team of equals unless there's a head on the chopping block. Then it's mine. Understood?" There were nods all around.

"Now, who's doing what. Charlie will be our liaison with SIOC."

"Sorry, Nathanial. What's SIOC?" asked Sam.

"Strategic Information and Operations Center. Charlie, you want to take this one?"

"Sure. This might surprise you, but even Headquarters used an ad hoc emergency operations center until the late 1980s. And we got caught with our pants down on 9/11. Suddenly we had to send resources to New York and DC, gather the intelligence we had on the most significant attack on US soil since Pearl Harbor, and ensure it didn't happen again. For sure, 9/11 changed everything in the intelligence game. And frankly, the FBI was not up to the job in 2001. But that changed quickly.

Overnight, counterterrorism went from one of a half-dozen priorities to the #1 priority. Every other case was pushed down the rung to make room for the new order. If there were ever an opportune time to commit a federal offense other than terrorism, 2001 would have been it. Thought I might take up bank robbing myself. Anyway, literally, every agent was assigned counterterrorism work. I was working on fraud, and that investigation got shoved in a drawer so fast it'd make your head spin. Congress pushed mountains of money at the FBI, CIA, NSA, and everyone else. And the FBI made the analyst position equal to the agent—which pissed off a lot of the old guard but was necessary. Anyway, that was when SIOC came into being. It's a 24/7 operation designed to be the nerve center of the FBI's most critical operations worldwide. They can be helpful. But they gotta be fed information and pointed in the right direction."

"Thanks, Charlie. We must keep feeding them information, so ensure you enter everything into CaseMaster. Speaking of, can you give Sam a quick how-to on that?"

"Yep."

"Ok, moving on. Terry is an experienced investigator and a lawyer, which is why his shirt is so nice." Terry rolled his eyes, but he was laughing too. "Terry and Sam are outside the FBI, although Terry has been inside it too. But you two, I want especially to question how we do things. Getting set in your ways is easy in a big institution, so keep asking questions. Terry's job is to investigate, to follow leads where they take him. We've already seen that Black NA students might feel more comfortable talking to you, which makes sense in a case like this. So, Terry, as much as possible, I want you to be in public. Eat lunch in the cafeteria. Walk around campus. Be available. Sound good?"

"I can do that for sure."

"Not to mention it'll annoy the shit out of Ralph Pelham."

Terry grinned.

"That's great. By the way, did you two get your secure FBI emails up and running yet?"

"Mine is," said Terry.

"I'm still waiting on mine, said Sam, "You know how it is when one bureaucracy has to talk to another. But they assured me it would be set up today."

"Ok, Sam, keep on them. I want us all in the loop, which brings me to Sam's role. Sam comes to us from NCIS, so she's also an investigator. And in some ways, it occurs to me is used to investigating her compatriots in a way the three of us aren't. Of course, anything related to the Marines or any military branch will run through Sam. Given this involves NA students, I think we will do a lot of liaising with the armed services for records and background. Ok, any questions? Let's get to work. We'll meet back here at 4 pm for our first daily after-action. That'll be a standing thing, by the way, so keep that in mind. Ok, everyone, let's get to work."

As Nathaniel returned to his office, he heard Charlie starting his CaseMaster speech for Sam.

The SIOC occupies over 40,000 square feet at FBI Headquarters on the fifth floor of the Hoover building at 10th and Pennsylvania Avenue and employs nearly 500 people. As a SCIF, a Sensitive Compartmentalized Information Facility, the SIOC offers a location to host classified briefings and gatherings to discuss the most sensitive information without fear of compromise by sophisticated foreign and terrorist collection devices. It also houses six crisis team action rooms and five principal rooms that permit the Bureau to coordinate multiple major sites simultaneously.

Sitting atop the command of this prodigious operation was Reginald "Reggie" Samuelson. A former pro linebacker in a dark suit, he was a Deputy Director of the Criminal Division—the FBI's premier division. Reggie was a no-nonsense guy who played by the rules. He liked law and order—with an emphasis on order. He prided himself on running a tight ship and did not like freelancers like Inspector Nathaniel Croft.

The lynching that had taken place on Monday had set FBIHQ spinning into action. Reggie had designated one of the six unique rooms as "Quantico Kill." He had assigned to that room several analysts, now a staple of the Bureau's response to major crimes, and two special agents coordinating crisis response teams collecting evidence and collating data that Charlie was sending in via CaseMaster. Video from news channels, interview reports from Quantico and other field offices, fingerprints, and DNA samples were dumped into this digital caldron to find out who did it and why. And while Charlie was in constant contact with the Headquarters team since the killing, Nathaniel considered the Headquarters' crisis team window-dressing for the media. The actual investigation was taking place within his team, not by a gaggle of geeks headed by the rule-bound, referee-type personality of Reggie Samuelson, a New Agent classmate of Nathaniel's and a genuine pain in Nathaniel's ass ever since.

While Nathaniel was eating a sandwich at his desk and reading over the interviews that had already been conducted, his cell phone rang. The Law-and-Order theme ringtone alerted him it was the Director, and he picked up, hurriedly swallowing.

"Croft."

"Inspector Croft, please wait for the Director."

"OK," he said, despising this Kabuki reverential phone dance.

"Nathaniel?"

"Yes, Director, and what might I do for you on this fine day?"

"Don't be a wise ass. I told you to coordinate with the head of SIOC and the Terrorism Assistant Director, who told me you have not."

"Can I guess which one called to tattle?"

"No need. Call Reggie and then Jaun Diaz in terrorism today, Nathaniel. It's called respect."

"R-E-S-P-E-C-T," he spelled out, "Aretha would be proud."

Then nothing but a dial tone on the other end of the call.

11
THE BRIEFING

Thursday, September 18

That afternoon at 4 PM, the team gathered for their daily after-action briefing. They assembled around a flip chart at the rear of the office in a space bounded by file cabinets.

The flip chart had their four names and four different colored sticky notes. There were four columns: Backlog. To Do. Doing. Done.

Nathaniel said, "OK, this is a Kanban board. It will track our team's process. Toyota used it to become a powerhouse in the auto industry. It will help us visualize our work and give each of us some accountability."

"Hmm," said Charlie, "Looks pretty, hope it works."

"It does; just ask GM and Ford about the impact of Toyota on them. We'll start with paper and convert it to the electronic board I requested. "

Sam nodded. "We were exposed to Kanban in E.W.S."

"What's E.W.S?" asked Terry.

"Sorry, sir. Expeditionary Warfare School, where the Corps trains its captains for advanced command."

Terry nodded. "Sam, remember you don't have to 'sir' anyone here."

"It will take me a while to get used to that."

Nathaniel continued. "OK, I want everyone to take a different color and write one task or idea per sticky note that describes work you need to get done, are doing, or have completed. For example,

I'll take the pink sticky note and write, 'Interviewed Rasheed's wife, Shari, and son, Randal, in Detroit.' Now, I'll put it under the column labeled: Done. All of my stickie notes will be pink." He wrote and put the sticky on the flip chart as he spoke.

"From that interview, I learned that Rasheed and other Black Marines had bad experiences with his platoon sergeant and lieutenant in Afghanistan. So, I will give Sam a task to find out who Rasheed's commanders were and dig up the other guys in his platoon to verify. Sam, what color do you want?"

"Um, yellow." Nathaniel wrote out the post-it and put it in Sam's column.

Charlie responded, "So basically, you're setting out leads for yourself and others."

"This is the rational version of the conspiracy theorist's wall with the red string. Like the It's Always Sunny in Philadelphia gif," said Sam.

Nathaniel and Terry laughed. Charlie looked baffled. "I'll show you later," whispered Sam.

"So not only is it a way to keep track of what you're doing, you can tell me what I should do, or I could even assign it to you and vice versa depending on how relevant it was to your current investigative path or branch. So now you all write down what you've done and what you or we must do to solve this case."

Sam took the yellow stickies, Charlie took the green ones, and Terry took the blue ones. As he did, he asked, "Can't we get someone to do this for us and save our valuable time for more important things?"

"Sir, I mean Nathaniel, if I might address Terry's question?" Sam asked.

Nathaniel nodded, and she continued. "Especially in the beginning, it's important for us to own it all. We learned in EWS that some tasks should never be delegated, especially when it requires expertise like yours."

Terry smiled briefly and said, "OK, I'll play along."

When the team was finished, there were lots of colored stickies all over the board. Nathaniel stood back to admire what they'd done. "Terry, tell us about this one," he said, pointing to the blue sticky he had placed under the "done" column. It read: "Interviewed Isaac Welty."

"Last night, I talked to a NA student named Isaac Welty, an African American cop from Detroit. The one I mentioned in the meeting with the Director."

Nathaniel raised his eyebrows.

Terry continued, "Welty had become friends with Mohammed Rasheed. They knew each other a little back in Detroit but got closer here. He emailed me because he'd seen my talk about my suit against the Bureau at the last NOBLE conference. Anyway, he said Rasheed could be a pain in the ass."

"Terry, what's NOBLE stand for?" asked Sam.

"NOBLE is the National Organization of Black Law Enforcement."

"Thanks."

"Welty gave me two white guys, Alex Roland, and Hershel Jones, weightlifters. And, this was an interesting tidbit: the morning Rasheed was killed, Isaac saw Roland returning from what he assumed was a workout dressed in black. He said it was out of character both in the timing and that Jones wasn't with him. Course, you would be sweaty after beating a man to death. I'm working on interviewing Roland today after his classes. He also hinted that Roland had a white supremacist tattoo removed from his bicep. I think that alone is worth finding out more."

Nathaniel interjected as he looked at the board, "I don't see a blue sticky under To Do. Can you add it now, so we can track what needs doing?"

Terry reluctantly started to write a sticky. "I asked Sam to do his background this morning."

Nathaniel started to move toward the board, but before he could, Sam said, "Sir, I put a yellow sticky under Done—background research on Alex Roland."

"Can we go sit down? I don't wanna take notes standing up like a reporter," Charlie grumbled.

Nathaniel laughed and motioned everyone back over to the desks. He pulled a rolling chair from a nearby desk and nodded at Sam.

She smiled, pulled out an iPad, and began. "Alex Roland. Grew up in River Rouge, Michigan, near Detroit—a small former manufacturing town that dried up. Used to be white working class, now mostly poor minorities. His father was an alcoholic and left when Alex was 10. Mother struggled financially. Alex got into some trouble. Hung out with skinhead friends and played Nazi punk stuff like the band Heil-H. Got tossed in jail for assault. A bunch of his gang severely beat up some Black kids."

Grimacing, Nathaniel injected, "Sounds like a nice wholesome all-American kid you'd want dating your daughter."

Sam nodded and continued. "The judge ordered Alex to join the Army as his get-out-of-jail-free pass. Did a three-year hitch. Then he joined the Wayne County Sheriff's department. Ends up in corrections. Starts lifting."

She paused to take a sip of coffee and turned the page. "Huge guy, 6'6", over 300 pounds, according to his file. Great record. Regular promotions. Gets early selection to the National Academy. Not much of a socializer but does well in class. I also did some work on Hershel Jones. He alibies out. Contacted his sister in Baltimore, who claims he was there all weekend. Skipped classes on Friday."

"Before I forget, Charlie, please send out a lead to the Baltimore field office to confirm the sister's comments."

"Trust but verify! Will do," he said, reaching for a sticky note to put on the board. "Ok, I gotta say something. Tell me if I'm off base here, but doesn't the over-the-top nature of this crime feel kinda off?"

"I've been thinking the same thing, especially once I read the autopsy file," said Terry. "Don't get me wrong; there's still a personal hatred to beat a man to death. And there may very well be a racial component to this crime. But real neo-Nazis carve the swastika into your chest and string you up while you're alive."

"Agreed. Not to mention that it's tough to be a member of a white supremacist group and get into the National Academy. The background checks are extensive," said Nathaniel. "This feels like a crime designed to attract maximum media attention and send everyone in the FBI into a tizzy."

"I agree, and I must also bring up the timing. I'm here because General Mathers is up for a confirmation hearing in two weeks. Is someone trying to throw a wrench into that process?"

"All good points, Sam. Ok, let's keep an open mind from now on. What's next, then?" asked Nathaniel.

Terry spoke up. "I'm setting up Roland's interview for 5:15 tonight. Charlie, can you sit in?"

"No problem."

"Ok, anything else? That's it for now. Terry, let me know how the interview goes. Sam, put a trace on Rasheed's military file. Find out what's hanging it up. Maybe it'll suddenly materialize if someone in uniform asks for it."

Nathaniel decided to do an encrypted video call to Reggie late that afternoon.

Reggie loved schedules and worked until 5 PM every day unless there was a serious crisis or the Director was swinging by for a tour, usually with a visiting dignitary. Nathaniel scheduled the call for 4:45. Decked out in an expensive suit as he sat in the teleconferencing center at the Academy, he looked like he was about to do the 7 PM news. On the other end, the figure of Reggie Samuelson appeared with his sleeves rolled up, his hands-on image. He spoke until Nathaniel put his hands up to his ears and squinted to say, "Huh?" Embarrassed, Reggie clicked on the speaker.

"Sorry about that. Nathaniel, how the hell are you and congrats on catching the Quantico case."

Nathaniel just rolled his eyes. "Yeah, and second prize is a set of steak knives!"

"Huh?"

"Just a line from Alex Baldwin in Glengarry Glen Ross. Just saying, not sure this is anything to brag about. But hey, I'm just calling to kiss your ring and make you feel good. The Director wants me to play nice, but then again, you know me."

"Still an asshole, I see."

"Why, thank you. That's the nicest name I've been called today. Look, Reggie, you and I won't ever be friends, ever since you dimed me off in new agents."

"Look, you were the one caught driving under the influence. I was just the duty agent. I was required."

"Reggie, leave it. And you're still a tattletale to the Director. Leopards don't change their spots. Look, Reggie, I'm officially coordinating with you, and Charlie has been working with the headquarters team, which I'm positive will solve the case in a couple of weeks or so, and we'll all head home."

"Nathaniel, we're a resource for you and your team and—"

"Yep, sure. Thanks, partner. Talk soon," and he hung up.

Nathaniel's next video call, at 5 pm, was to Juan Diaz. He was a few years younger than Nathaniel, a short Cuban-American who was razor-sharp. A Yale Law degree and a laid-back personality had catapulted him to the head of the Counterterrorism Division.

When Nathaniel appeared on video, Juan was already there—looking as crisp as ever and sipping a drink from a glass.

"Am I speaking to the Assistant Director of the FBI's Counter Terrorism Division?"

"No, sir, but let me get him."

They both laughed. They'd been friends for years since they attended an in-service for new senior executives.

"And I do hope that glass has some alcohol in it."

Juan looked at his watch and said, "It is 5 PM."

"OK, this is my official call. The Director was all over my ass that I hadn't checked in yet, but I know Charlie has been talking to your guys, and he's the best."

"Yep, no problem on my end. We got nada. You and I both know this isn't some Neo-Nazi terrorism case. Somebody wanted this guy gone. I think he was a bit of a dick, which got him offed by someone with a specific motive, not some wild Heil-Hitler nut job."

"Bingo. That's why you're the AD of Terrorism—Counter Terrorism. "

"Here for you, buddy, when you need anything," he said, hoisting his glass up as a mock toast.

"Be well," Nathaniel said, hitting the "End Meeting for All" button on the video call.

As Nathaniel finished his video calls, Terry and Charlie set up in a room across campus. The rooms that the New Agent's Training Unit used for interview and interrogation exercises were particularly compact but realistic: A table with two chairs behind and one chair in front of a bare desk. Phone on the wall. Pretty stark. These were not rooms designed to make you comfortable, as anyone who'd sat on those chairs knew.

Typically, the new agents interviewed seasoned actors, who were hired on contract to act in a prescribed role, and then adapt after they saw the reaction of the new agent to exchanges between them. One key concept they learned was the difference between an interview, which focuses on gaining information, and an interrogation, which determines the truth or deception. And finally, determining what that deception is based on. Sometimes it was direct involvement; other times, guilty knowledge, like covering for a friend or family member.

The wall clock read 6:15 PM when Roland darkened the door like a solar eclipse. He took up most of the doorframe. In fact, he instinctively ducked to make sure his head cleared the doorframe—something he was no doubt used to.

He entered the room and sat awkwardly in the only chair left. It faced into the room, so he had to sit with his back to the door, a position designed to make him uncomfortable.

Terry looked at the clock and said, "You have trouble finding the room?"

"Nope."

"Well, at least you made it. I'm Agent Terry Jamison, and this is Agent Charlie Thompson. We're investigating the death of Mohammed Rasheed. Do you mind if we record this interview?" Alex showed no reaction and offered no comment. He looked up at the clock and tapped his fingers.

"You have somewhere to go tonight, Alex?"

"Nope."

Terry shot Charlie a quick look and asked, "OK. Where were you between 5 and 6 AM on May 1st—the morning Rasheed was killed?"

"The gym."

"OK. I'll bite. What were you doing in the gym so early?"

"Lifting."

"Look, Alex, how about more than one word at a time, or we'll be here all night."

"OK. Lifting weights."

Charlie almost laughed but controlled it by faking a cough.

"A little on the early side for you to lift in the morning?"

"Yep."

"You want to elaborate on that?"

"Nope."

"Anyone else there who can verify that's where you were?"

"Nope."

"When did you leave the gym?"

"At 6."

"Did you see anything unusual on your way to or from the gym?"

"Nope."

"You have any idea who killed Rasheed?"

"Nope."

Terry was exasperated as he turned to Alex. "To sum it up, you were lifting weights by yourself at 5 AM, leaving the gym at about 6 AM and returning to the dorm. That's about right? Oh, yeah, and you have no idea what happened to Mohammed Rasheed."

"Yep."

Terry's eyes widened as he looked at Charlie and then back at Alex. "OK. Last question of the night, Alex. Will you take a polygraph?"

"Yep."

"OK, Alex. Thank you SO much. We'll be back in touch."

After Alex had lumbered out the door, Terry slammed his pen on the table.

"Well, that was a giant waste of time."

"Never seen a guy answer questions like he was being charged by the letter," said Charlie.

"Well, I'm off. I need a drink. Will you fill in Nathaniel, or shall I?"

"Do you mind? I'm headed back to the office to install the camera. See if we can catch our spy."

"Right. See you tomorrow then."

Charlie decided to grab dinner in the canteen before he installed the camera to ensure the cleaners had come and gone, so it was late and dark inside the task force office when he arrived. Charlie stood on a chair, reaching through a ceiling tile he'd slipped back. He started to adjust the small fish-eye camera when suddenly, he heard footsteps and saw a beam of light.

Startled, he nearly fell off his chair but managed to get the ceiling tile back in time to get down and hide under a vacant desk in the back of the room. Someone turned a key in the office lock and entered. The intruder walked into Nathaniel's office, then to Charlie's desk, rooted through the drawers, then left. Charlie waited a few minutes, then got up and turned on his computer to check the camera feed. It was running but not well-focused. Charlie quickly dialed the phone.

"Nathaniel, we had a visitor tonight in the office."

"Who?"

"Can't tell yet. I'd barely set the thing up, so it's blurry. But we'll be ready next time."

At 6:30 PM that night, Sam got into her red Miata convertible and drove out of the Academy grounds and onto MCB-1—the main drag that leads to route 95. The top was down, her hair was blowing, and Reba McEntire singing "Consider Me Gone" was blasting from the speakers. It was a beautiful fall night, and she was in a good place. She cruised along at 48 miles per hour; she liked to keep it under five over the limit.

Suddenly, out of nowhere, a marked Military Police (MP) car with flashing lights on pulled out from a wooded area. Sam slowed to 44, certain he was headed after someone else. Still, the MP bore down on her with his flashers on, so she pulled over, more as a gesture to let him by. But he pulled up right behind her. An electric shot of fear ran through her gut, wondering what could be the matter.

The MP sat in his car for a while, first talking on the radio and writing something down. Then he approached her vehicle.

"Evening, Captain. May I please see your license and registration?"

"Why? What's the matter?"

"You were doing 61 in a 45-mile-an-hour zone."

"I was doing exactly 48—just three over the limit."

"Captain, may I please see your license and registration."

She handed over her license and registration to the officer.

He took it all back to his car and wrote it up.

She sat fuming and glanced in her rear-view mirror periodically. Finally, she saw him coming back and readied herself.

He handed back her license, registration, and a ticket.

"Ma'am, I've given you a speeding ticket for doing 61 in a 45-mile-per-hour zone, which is considered reckless driving. And in accordance with the Uniform Code of Military Justice, you will have to appear in a court-martial appearance. I suggest you contact the Judge Advocate's Office for representation."

"Reckless! A court-marshal offense! Are you kidding me? I was only doing 48!"

"Thank you, Captain. Have a nice night."

He walked away, got into his car, and pulled off.

Sam pounded the steering wheel. She looked at her watch and realized she'd be late to meet Marge for dinner. She drove the rest of the way to The Lazy Pig, keeping carefully to the speed limit.

Sam and Marge had become fast friends. They were the only two women living on their floor at the Bachelor Officer Quarters, known as the BOQ, and Marge had shown Sam around Quantico. As Sam entered the low-key BBQ restaurant, Marge waved to her from a table by the window.

"You'll never believe what just happened!" fumed Sam as she sat down. "I got a speeding ticket that said I was doing 61, but I was only doing 48! That's a court-martial offense for reckless driving."

"Some MP with a quota, no doubt. Listen, go talk to Sergeant Major Wilson tomorrow and explain the situation. He'll sort it out. And if you need a lawyer, you've got me. In the meantime, you look like you could use a bourbon," said Marge as she flagged down their waitress.

"Y'all ready to order?"

"Yes, ma'am. The pulled pork dinner for me, with mac and cheese, green beans, and cornbread. And a sweet tea."

"Brisket dinner for me, mac and cheese, coleslaw, cornbread, and a sweet tea. Thanks." The waitress bustled away, and Sam said, "I wish they had a bar here."

"Me too, but I'm sure the prospect of hordes of drunk jarheads keeps them from getting one. Anyway, tell me everything about the task force! Or is that all need-to-know? Are there code words? Do you have an alias? Come on, feed my James Bond fantasy, please."

Sam laughed. "Well, I could tell you about the new top-secret tech, but then I'd have to kill you."

The waitress set down two tall glasses of sweet tea on the table and bustled away. Marge produced a pint flask of Jack Daniels and poured a hearty slug into each glass.

"Marge!"

"What? You said you wanted some bourbon. I was a Girl Scout before I was a Marine and took 'Be Prepared' seriously."

"Marge, that's the Boy Scout motto," said Sam, taking a hearty sip.

"It's the Girl Scout motto too! And trust me, if you need a campfire built, you want a Girl Scout. So, Marine, scouting report. Any eligible bachelors on the task force?"

"There are two single men. At least two men without rings. How dateable either one remains to be seen. It's only been a day!"

"Listen, it's not that I don't love being neighbors with you. But being at the BOQ as a divorcee is depressing. I used to have a house! And now I live like a college kid. I'm 44. It's unnatural."

Sam laughed, and the waitress set down their plates.

"I mean, I don't need to get married again immediately, possibly ever. But I must spend a few nights a week, not at the BOQ. And I've sworn off Marines. Not all of them take 'semper fi' literally."

"You know," said Sam as she spread butter on her cornbread, "I hadn't been thinking much about dating. But now that you frame it that way…."

"Picture it, Sam: a non-single bed! The ability to have coffee in your bathrobe!"

"I'll have to update my Hinge profile. One of my prompts can be 'Wanted: a man with a queen-sized bed, good coffee maker, and plush bathrobe. No Marines need to apply.'"

"Oh god, I'm gonna have to get on the apps, aren't I? It's bad enough I have an old lady's name. I don't even know what Hinge is."

"I'll show you the ropes! I owe you after all the tricks you showed me at Quantico. Plus, it's not that different than online dating."

"Oh, it was my pleasure. And I have to confess that I never did online dating."

"Marge! What??"

"Sam, the last time I was single, the iPhone hadn't even been invented."

"Oh… wow."

"I know it's hard to believe. And I can see you doing math in your head. Hey, do you still want to go up to DC this weekend? The Air and Space Museum is next on our list of Smithsonians. This might be my last weekend before work gets intense."

"Oh my god, is that where Amelia Earhart's plane is? I've been dying to see it. She made me want to be a pilot as a kid."

"Me too! Is your eyesight also not good enough to be a pilot? That was a crushing blow when I joined up."

"No, I've got great eyes. Highest vision score in my class. But it turns out the flight harnesses trigger my claustrophobia. Had a full-on freakout in the cockpit and punched the instructor, trying to get me out. Super embarrassing."

"What's Basic if you don't humiliate yourself at least once? We can't all be Amelia. But we can go see her plane."

"And trade theories about what happened to her on the drive?"

"You giant nerd! Yes, of course, we can. Did you see that documentary that came out last year?"

Sam was much better when she and Marge left the restaurant.

"See you back at the ranch for a nightcap?" Marge asked as they walked to their cars.

"I'd love to, but I've got to talk to Sergeant Major Wilson about my ticket before I report to the task force office at 0900. Rain check?"

"You know where to find me and my buddy Jack if you need us," said Marge with a wink.

12
FUEL

Friday, September 19

Sam's alarm went off as usual at 6 am, and she was warming up for her morning run outside the BOQ by 6:15. Running was her thinking time, and she usually did her daily run without headphones. She liked the quiet of the early morning, the mist off the Potomac, and the steady rhythm of her feet against the ground. She had planned to see the Sergeant Major about her speeding ticket on the way to the task force office, but the more she thought about it, the more she was sure Wilson would want an update on the task force. Before she talked to him, she needed to confer with Nathaniel. It was going to be a tricky balancing act to serve two masters.

When Sam walked into the task force office at 8 am, she was surprised to see everyone else settling in at their desks. Charlie was busy checking the tape under his desk drawer, and Terry was plugging in a Keurig coffee machine on a table by the door.

"Terry, is that what I think it is??"

"Yes, ma'am, it is. Any investigation needs fuel, and I have lost my taste for government sludge. Ditto the powdered creamer, so there's a minifridge under here. Plenty of room for snacks or lunches too."

"Terry, you absolute angel!"

"Would you like to do the honors, Sam?"

"Well, someone has to go first, I suppose." She popped a pod into the machine and hit start.

"Terry, I was going to make fun of you and your champagne tastes, but that smells so good I'll just say 'thank you,'" said Charlie. Terry rolled his eyes as he passed Charlie a mug.

Nathaniel wandered out of his office and beamed.

"Well, now I'd say the task force is complete."

Sam started to laugh as they stood around with their freshly-made coffees, chatting about the case.

"What's so funny, Sam?" asked Nathaniel.

"All those courses on unit cohesion I took in the EWS, and it turns out all it takes is a decent coffee machine." Everyone laughed at that and then strolled back to their desks.

"Sir, uh, I mean Nathaniel, can I talk to you briefly?"

"Of course, Sam." She followed him into his office.

"I got a speeding ticket last night on the base, and I need to talk to Sergeant Major Wilson about it. The radar gun must have been faulty because it had me going 61 in a 45 rather than the 48 I was driving. Anyway, I'm sure he will want an update on the task force. What can I tell him? Honor and integrity are important to me, so I won't lie. But I also understand that what we're doing here is very sensitive and need to know. I'm asking you as the leader of this unit. But I have to make my own decision about exactly what I say."

"I appreciate that, Sam. You're on a tightrope, and I don't envy you. Before I answer your question, let me ask one of my own. Is it true that the Sergeant Major's main concern is getting the general through his confirmation hearings, and thus wants this wrapped up ASAP?"

"I would agree with that."

"So, tell him we're interviewing two possible suspects, both NA students, and that one has agreed to a polygraph, and you'll let him know the results."

"I'm also going to ask him about Rasheed's military file. I'll say we're getting files on everyone involved in the case to see if there are any connections."

"Excellent idea. And we are, so it's the truth."

"Thanks, Nathaniel. Mind if I go see him now?"

"Not at all. Thanks, Sam."

Sam walked into Sergeant Major Wilson's office twenty minutes later. Marge, already at her desk, smiled at her as she walked by. The office hummed with activity with the general's confirmation hearing fast approaching. Marge was a lawyer with Congressional Affairs, and it was part of her job to help ensure the general's testimony was accurate and to help him prepare. They'd be starting mock questioning any day now, and Marge would be acting as the senator asking the questions.

Sam walked into Wilson's office. He kept working but looked up when he heard her getting closer. "So, Captain, how's the FBI investigation coming?"

"It's progressing."

She reached into her bag to pull out the ticket. "Sergeant Major, what's the procedure for traffic tickets on this base?"

He flashed a quizzical look. "Why?"

"I got one last night."

"No big deal. Could you give it to me? I process all tickets for the office."

She handed the ticket to him.

He read it carefully and looked up with concern. "Reckless driving. That's a different situation."

"I was doing 48 in a 45-mile-an-hour zone. This MP is either on a quota or his equipment's screwed up."

Wilson stared at the ticket and said, "I'll talk to the Gunnery

Sergeant in charge of enforcement at the Provost's Office. See if I can get him to, well, adjust it."

"If you can legally, ask him to check the equipment. I know something is off."

He smiled and winked at her.

"I'm sure they'll find some problem. Anything you can tell me about the investigation? It's important to the General."

"We've got two potential suspects, both National Academy students. The one they've already interviewed has agreed to take a polygraph, and they plan to interview the other guy ASAP. Sir, it sounds like Rasheed wasn't well-liked. Possibly there will be more suspects as things progress."

"And what do they have you doing?"

"Lots of background. I am pulling files on all those involved. I'm supposed to trace the victim's military personnel file. I called the National Personal Records Center in St. Louis to get them to release it to me because it's still a paper file, but they're having trouble locating it. Any suggestions?"

"If they can't find it in the next day or two, let me know, and I'll call. Anything else?"

"No, Sergeant Major."

"Thanks, Captain. And I'll call my friend about your ticket."

"Good. Thanks, Sergeant Major."

After she left, Wilson picked up his cell and shot off a quick text: Gimme a call asap—we got a problem.

13
TRUTH OR CONSEQUENCE

Friday, September 19

The polygraph room at the Academy was built to train aspiring polygraph examiners. To even be selected for the examiner's course, the agent had to have been a master interviewer with a reputation for getting confessions. Indeed, getting criminals to admit the truth about their unlawful behavior was the coin of the realm when it came to interviewing. Interviewing was intended to collect information, but when that information turned to deception, the interviewer's job was to switch to interrogation to determine the truth and why the person was being deceptive. The best agents made this switch deftly. And the best of the best became polygraph examiners, who were called in on significant cases. Each field office had at least one examiner, who was a breed apart.

Today, the examiner wasn't a student but the Bureau's most experienced agent-examiner from the Polygraph Unit at FBI Headquarters. Special Agent Patricia Helden was 45 and had served in several field offices with great distinction. She had interviewed mass murderers, extortionists, kidnappers, white-collar criminals, terrorists, and a litany of bad actors in Chicago, LA, Miami, and New York. She was a deceptively small and slight Black woman with close-cropped hair and horned-rimmed glasses that made her look more like a librarian than an FBI agent. Her voice was soft, measured, and confident. And while her physical presence was unthreatening, at one time, she had held almost all of the FBI's fitness records for female agents going through the Academy—from pullups to pushups to sit-ups to the two-mile run. And she was ferocious on the mats, having studied martial arts her whole life, no doubt in response to larger, dumber bullies she'd encountered. In short, while Pat was easy to underestimate, doing so was a huge mistake, which many criminals and even other agents, especially male agents, had made.

The room was stark and empty except for the polygraph chair, with its extra-long flat arms, another single chair, and a table. There was a sizeable two-way mirror facing the hot seat. On the other side was an observation room where Nathaniel, Terry, and Charlie sat. Sam would join them after she spoke to Wilson.

The polygraph laptop was ready with all its wires and tubes atop the flat-top desk behind which Pat sat, making a few adjustments when Roland banged on the door frame. Pat stood up to welcome him into the room. "Hello, you must be Mr. Roland," she said, extending her right hand. He gave her a chin nod but ignored the handshake and headed toward the chair.

"Please have a seat, Mr. Roland. May I call you Alex?"

He nodded yes and sat in the examinee's chair at a right angle to the examiner's chair. Pat moved her chair to face Alex.

"Great, thank you, Alex. Today we're going to be talking about your relationship with Mohammad Rasheed. I will ask you a series of questions, and you'll answer them to the best of your ability. You've already signed the waiver, so we can start if you're ready."

He nodded yes.

"Before we connect you to the machine, I will give you an overview of how this will go so you're comfortable. I'll ask some substantive questions like, 'did you know Mr. Rasheed'? I'll also ask simple baseline questions like 'do you live in Michigan?'"

Alex Roland barely fit in the polygraph chair. Two rubber pneumatic tubes with special extensions strained across his massive chest and abdomen to track his respiration. A black blood pressure cuff strained across his massive biceps despite a special extender. Two finger cots with metal contacts covered the tips of Alex's left index and ring finger to record his sweat.

Pat looked at the screen monitor that recorded Alex's bodily functions in response to strictly yes-or-no questions.

"OK, Alex, we've discussed the nature and reason for this polygraph. For the record, you've stated that this is a voluntary examination—meaning that you can terminate the process anytime you like. Furthermore, the polygraph is not admissible in court."

Alex nodded.

"Fine, then, let's start with a simple test of the system." Pat handed Alex a small piece of paper and a pen. "Please write a number from one to ten on the paper, fold it, and put it in your pocket for now. I will ask you ten brief questions about that number. Please answer no to all of them."

Alex looked puzzled but nodded.

"OK, is the number you wrote 1?"

"No."

Is the number you wrote 2?"

"No."

This process went on through the number 10. At this time, Pat turned the laptop monitor around and showed Alex the various lines, including one more erratic than all the others.

"So, I believe that the number you lied about was number 7. Please pull out the piece of paper with your selection."

Alex placed the folded piece of paper on the table. Pat opened it to expose a big "7" in the middle. Alex looked at it and stared ahead, unmoved by the obvious scare tactic.

"OK then, let's get started. We'll start with yes or no questions."

Alex nodded.

"Ok, first question: Is Alex Rolland your name?

"Yes."

Pat read the graph, which looked normal. No big spikes or valleys. She marked the chart on her computer with a stylus.

"Are you a Wayne County Sheriff's Department deputy sheriff?"

"Yes."

"Did you see Mohammed Rasheed on the morning of April 30?"

"No."

The digital line jumped outside the limits she'd marked as normal for Alex. She marked the end of that question and made a note.

"Did you ever harm Mohammed Rasheed?"

Pat riveted her attention on the screen.

"No."

Digital ink sprayed out of normal range—again—and Pat noted it.

"OK, Alex. Stay here for a few minutes. I'll be back.

Pat exited the room with the laptop and entered an adjacent soundproofed room with a one-way mirror. Nathaniel, Terry, and Charlie sat watching the show. "He's lying on the last two questions," Pat said.

Charlie piped up, "Ya think?"

Nathaniel tried not to laugh, and even Terry smiled.

Pat said straight-faced, "That's why they pay me the big bucks, Charlie."

Nathaniel sobered. "OK. Now what?"

Pat adjusted her glasses and said, "I'll take it from here."

She picked up a thick FBI file labeled "Alex Roland" on the cover they'd constructed from blank paper before the examination. After entering the examination room, Pat dropped the file on the desk with a thud, turned around the monitor, and took off her glasses. "Alex, you have what in my business we call a BFP—a big fucking problem."

She pointed to the first several questions on his charts.

In the observation room, Nathaniel, Charlie, and Terry looked at each other like someone had just farted in church.

Alex grunted as he looked at the screen.

Pat pointed to the screen. “Here you're telling the truth. Your name, where you work. See?”

She didn't wait for an answer.

“But HERE, where I asked if you saw Rasheed on the 30th, and HERE—” she pointed to another part of the screen, “I asked if you ever harmed him. Well, partner, YOU lied like a rug. Maybe you had a good reason. Maybe he hit you, or maybe—”

Alex stared at Pat and erupted: "Bullshit.”

Pat got within two inches of Alex's face, stared back at him, and declared, “You lied—period. So, you want to explain it?”

Alex looked poised to launch off the chair like a missile.

“You leave now, and you'll look guilty as hell. Your best bet is to explain yourself. Let me ask you some more questions. Can you do that?”

Alex nodded.

“Ok, take a deep breath. Here we go. Did you ever hurt Mohammed Rasheed?”

Alex paused, looked toward the two-way mirror, and said, “Yes.”

A couple of blips, but the needles stayed in the normal range.

Pat didn't react but continued to make notes.

“Did you have anything to do with the murder of Mohammed Rasheed?”

Without hesitation, Alex answered: “No.”

Again, the charts looked normal.

Pat looked at the screen one more time and nodded her head. Then she left Alex to join Nathaniel and the others.

Alex sat and waited, exhausted but relieved.

Inside the observation room, Pat said, “He's telling the truth. Just need to find out how and when he hurt Rasheed.”

After taking a few minutes for dramatic effect, Pat sat down and leaned in as she began. "OK, Alex, everything looks good. So, tell me about when you hurt Mohammed Rasheed."

Alex tightened and looked toward the mirror.

"Rasheed's cousin was an inmate in our jail. His name was Albert Brown. He got in a fight. I jumped in. It kept Brown from getting his ass kicked. My uniform sleeve got torn and showed an old Aryan Nations tatt. Look, I was a kid when I got wrapped up in that shit."

"OK. Go on."

"After I save his ass, Brown starts calling me a racist."

"So I," he looked at the two-way mirror, "I tuned him up. Slapped him a couple of times. Told him to knock off the racist bullshit, or I'd kick his ass myself."

Pat nodded.

"One day, Rasheed comes to talk to me. He's a Detroit cop. And he's an even bigger asshole than his cousin. Goes off on some Afghanistan racism shit."

"Then what happened?"

"He got in my face. I could feel the spit off his mouth. He bumped me, so I grabbed him by the collar and lifted him off his feet and told him to shut the fuck up, or I'd kick his ass too. He started yapping about Internal Affairs, all that bullshit. Nothin' ever came of it. Never saw him again 'til he showed up here at the FBI Academy. Never touched him since then."

"OK, Alex, I believe you. But I want to ask you one more question with the polygraph running. OK?"

"OK."

Pat looked at Alex and asked: "Do you know who killed Mohammed Rasheed?"

"No."

Pat looked down at the screen, then back at Alex, and said, "OK, you're good to go."

Sam arrived just as the other three were getting ready to leave. "What'd I miss?"

"It's not Roland. We're back to square one," said Nathaniel.

"Well, shit."

"Took the words right out of my mouth, Sport," Charlie added.

14
TRUTH BE TOLD

Friday, September 19

At a quiet Italian restaurant just off the base, Avery Wilson and Ralph Pelham sat across from each other, eating the lasagna for which this eatery was legendary. When Ralph reached over to sip his glass of chianti, Wilson seized the opportunity. "Look, Ralph, I just talked to Captain Melton. She said there was some information about you that surfaced. Somethin' racial."

"What?" Ralph said, putting down his wine glass.

"They found some evidence about racial prejudice or somethin' at the Academy. Referred it to some internal investigators."

"OPR?"

"What?"

"The Office of Professional Responsibility?" Pelham asked with a laser stare.

"Yeah, yeah, that's it."

"Shit. They're the Bureau's Gestapo. What else did she say?"

"That's it, Ralph. And it ain't good."

Pelham looked at his watch, "Look, Avery. I need to get back. If you hear anything else, let me know ASAP. Right now, you've got a better source at my Academy than I do."

Pelham slammed down his napkin and left.

Wilson nodded goodbye but stayed to finish his meal. Wilson said when the waiter brought the check, "You can put that on Mr. Pelham's tab." He left without leaving a tip.

☆

In addition to the more exciting parts Charlie had shown Sam on her Academy tour, he'd shown her the FBI gym complex, which had state-of-the-art workout equipment available 24/7. Rooms full of bikes, treadmills, ellipticals, rowing machines, you name it. There was also a spacious weight room with a sea of machines and free weights, filled with grunting and groaning agents and Academy students trying to outdo each other.

After their only suspect evaporated, Nathaniel needed a workout to refocus. Keeping fit was essential to him. If his body was in shape, his mind felt sharp too. Like Sam with her daily run, he used the gym to think without thinking, letting his conscious mind focus on reps while his subconscious worked on whatever problem was plaguing him. He was a long way from the rowing crew at Stanford, but there was still no better place than a scull to sort out a thorny problem. He wasn't wild about using the FBI gym because it often turned into a macho lifting contest, but while on this case, he knew he wouldn't see the inside of the Equinox near his condo or the beauty of the Potomac at dawn as he rowed through the mist. A lunchtime workout would have to do.

After quickly changing into his black Under Armor shorts, t-shirt, and trusty Nikes, Nathaniel took two 25-pound weights to warm up. He stretched, moved to the bench, loaded a hundred pounds onto the silver barbell, and pulled on his black leather lifting gloves. Every eye scanned the weight and registered it. As he got himself situated under the bar, he rolled his eyes. Nathaniel had been on stage before, so he preferred his private gym. He gripped the bar as one might prepare for an arm-wrestling contest in a bar. When his fingers were well situated, he found his legs on either side of the bench, pulled back his shoulder blades, and then slowly, smoothly did eight reps.

Nathaniel then loaded on two 25-pound weights, squared away his shoulders, and pumped out eight more reps. He was warming up, and a few nearby lifters were watching, pretending to take a water break.

He swapped out the 25s for two 50-pound plates and cranked out five more like the others, smooth and slow. Now it was getting interesting.

Then he stopped to towel off, drink water, and walk around. That's when he took the weight up to 250. At this point, everyone watched without embarrassment as he climbed below the bar after asking a lifter nearby to spot him.

He made the first rep look hard for dramatic effect. Then, he cranked out five more as smoothly as he'd done before. Several of the cops looked at each other.

Nathaniel sat up, thanked his spotter, a pleasant, admiring NA student, and then his jaw dropped as he spotted Charlie.

"Quick, Dorothy, get Toto and Aunty Em and head for the storm cellar! It's the end of the world! Charlie Thompson in a gym?"

Charlie looked like he had just raided a Goodwill store: ancient Ohio Buckeyes basketball shorts and a T-shirt that had once been white. Only his New Balances were crisp. He glanced at Nathaniel and casually threw him the finger as he approached. "So, this is a gym?"

"Indeed, it is. You buy new shoes for the occasion?"

"I'm an old man, Nathaniel. I own comfortable footwear."

Nathaniel rolled his eyes. "Jesus, Charlie, you're 55, not 85." He squinted at Charlie's thin frame. "Your doctor didn't get on your case, did he?"

"No, Mommy, I just thought I'd get back in the PT groove a bit. That ok with you?"

"I'm thrilled. OK, I'm done lifting, but I was going to do some reps on the rowing machine. Want to join me?"

"Can't think of anything I'd rather do," grumbled Charlie as he followed Nathaniel out of the room. When they reached the hallway, Charlie asked, "Do I see things, or were half the guys in there watching you? You a celebrity or something, hotshot?"

Nathaniel sighed. "This is why I hate working out here. Rowing is an upper-body sport; I lift a lot. At least some meathead didn't challenge me to a duel this time."

"Yeah, yeah, it's tough being you."

"OK, while we're chatting, what the hell's going on? This is my first time seeing you around a bar that didn't serve booze."

"You can blame that Marine. I gave her a tour of Quantico on her first day, and she got excited about trying the Yellow Brick Road. Next thing you know, she's got me saying I'll go for a run with her. Well, it'll be fucking embarrassing if I keel over after five minutes, so I figured I better get active. You know I used to play a lot of hoops, but when Dianne got sick. Anyway, will you show me how to use one of these infernal machines or what?"

Twenty minutes later, Charlie was breathing hard but satisfied. "I can't believe I'm gonna say this, but that was… fun?"

Nathaniel laughed. "One of these days, I'll get you out into a boat with me. Now that's fun."

"One step at a time, Sport. I'm from the Midwest. We don't trust boats."

Nathaniel looked at his watch. "I lifted already, but I've got some time if you want me to walk you through the weight machines."

"I guess. But if I can't get out of bed tomorrow, it's your damn fault."

Charlie settled into the hip abduction machine. "I remember this one. I searched the database this morning and found a reference to Rasheed in the security logs just after he got to the Academy."

Charlie moved over to the chest machine, sat down, and talked through the equipment to Nathaniel. "Anyway, Danny Bode, a good old boy who runs the Academy garage, responded to a call when Rasheed broke down just off 95 on his way back to the Academy from DC."

"So?" Nathaniel asked as he moved behind Charlie and straightened up Charlie's posture to help him execute the exercise correctly. Charlie grunted out a couple more pull-downs.

"According to the complaint, Rasheed spotted a confederate flag decal on Danny's government truck and started going off on him… after Danny fixed his flat."

Charlie had moved to the parson's bench to do some bicep curls. He tried to remember how this odd-looking machine worked—like a guy trying to remember how to tie a bow tie for a formal. Again, Nathaniel helped him position himself correctly, adjusting Charlie's posture. "Rasheed talked trash about the South, confederates, racism. Well, you can imagine how that went over. So, Rasheed reports Danny having the confederate decal on a government vehicle. It turns out it was an open secret around the academy, but now it was an official complaint."

"What the hell was he doing with a confederate flag on a government vehicle? That's an unforced error if ever I've seen one."

"I'll say. OPR investigated and found that the complaint had merit. But like all investigations, OPR stirred up some extra crap. Good-ole-boy Danny has been moonlighting, running an illegal repair operation out of the Bureau garage, using Bureau tools and even Bureau parts. It ends up being a real shit storm for Danny."

"Hmm, the plot thickens."

"Yep. OPR shut down Danny's side hustle, which he claimed was a college fund for his son. A whole sob story about it."

"So let me get this straight: his side hustle was getting the unsuspecting taxpayer to subsidize his kid's education. You know they have an actual program for that. It's called the Pell Grant."

"Think we need to talk to our industrious entrepreneur?"

"I'll say. That's motive if ever I've heard one. Let's go find Danny."

"I've had as much gym fun as I can stand today. Let's go to work."

After quick showers, Nathaniel and Charlie walked out the gym's back door, where runners left to hit the surrounding trails around the Academy—no doubt the way Rasheed had left for the last time. They walked about 100 meters into a huge outbuilding: the Academy garage. The place was pristine, with four bays, well-ordered tools, and a floor that squeaked under Charlie's rubber soles. In one bay stood a large muscular guy, wearing a full beard and sporting various tattoos. He had just broken down a large truck tire and tossed it into a recycle bin like a broken toy. He looked in their general direction but paid little attention to Charlie and Nathaniel as they headed for Danny Bode's office.

Danny was in his late 40s, wiry and thin, with salt and pepper hair, and was busy doing paperwork in the small glassed-in office inside the garage. An outdated girly calendar hung from one of the walls, a bunch of parts, some in boxes, and assorted piles of other junk cluttered the cramped grease monkey's office. He was writing on an invoice form as they approached.

"Danny Bode?" asked Nathaniel.

Danny looked up, startled, and nodded yes.

After flipping out his credentials, Nathaniel said, "Danny, I'm Nathaniel Croft, and this is Charlie Thompson. We're working on the Rasheed murder case. Wonder if you could help us?"

Danny nodded as he fidgeted with his pen.

Nathaniel noticed that Danny's pen had a pretty woman who turned naked whenever Danny turned the pen upside down. Charlie also saw and gave Nathaniel a side glance as he pulled out his pad and pen to take notes on the interview.

Nathaniel took the lead. "Can you tell me what you know about Mohammed Rasheed?"

"Not much. NA student," Danny replied as he nervously fingered the pen. Charlie took notes and watched the woman get half undressed and then dressed again, the cycle incomplete because Danny flipped the pen so quickly.

"Ever talk to him?"

Danny fidgeted with the pen even more now, which made the woman in the pen look like an exotic dancer on fast-forward. The sounds of the garage filled the place —air guns screaming, tools clanking, engines revving.

"Can't remember. They's so many come through here."

Nathaniel gave him a hard stare. "Danny, think real hard. Maybe about the night you were called out to pick him up. Black guy. Had a flat. Remarked about your confederate flag."

Danny looked down at his pen, "Damn. Yeah, NOW I remember. Didn't like the confederate flag on my truck."

Nathaniel walked closer to Danny. Then he sat in a chair nearer him, got on his level, scooted close to Danny, leaned in, and said. "Danny, let's fast forward. Rasheed reported you. OPR investigated. You lost your side business."

Danny slammed down the pen. His eyes narrowed, and his teeth clenched. Then he spit out with venom, "Yeah, I knew that N.... that bastard. I tried to help that asshole and got fucked, all 'cause of a confederate flag. In Virginia? Shit!"

Nathaniel's tone became more sympathetic as he worked with Danny, "You have every right to be angry. I'd be pissed too. We're just now finding out what a piece of work Rasheed was."

"Hey Danny, we got— oh shit, didn't realize you had company." One of Danny's mechanics looked sheepish.

"Hey, Eddie. I'll come to find you in a minute." Eddie hurried from the office.

"Yeah, OPR shut down my bi'ness 'cause of that asshole. My kids' college money. Motherfucker."

"Got to make you mad."

"You bet."

"Mad enough to do something about it?"

Danny suddenly saw where this conversation was headed. His face turned bright red, and he stood up now with pen in hand, like it was a weapon.

"Look, this guy was an asshole, but I ain't done a thing to him, 'cept we had a few words the night I helped him out. That's all. Goddamn it."

Nathaniel stood up, towering over Danny, and looked down at him. "Then you won't mind taking a polygraph exam. Right?"

Danny started fidgeting with the pen again. Then he said, "Hell, yes. I'll take a polygraph. Son of a bitch! Try to help someone. Do a Christian deed and get screwed blue! Shit."

Charlie looked up from his notes and noticed Danny playing with the pen again.

"Oh, by the way," said Nathaniel, "what time do you open the shop in the morning?"

"7-ish, why?"

"Just curious. We'll schedule a polygraph for you in the next day or so. By the way, we might want to talk to more of your guys, so let them know they need to be available to us. Thanks."

Nathaniel and Charlie left. Danny threw the pen at the desk. Now the woman was covered up completely. After leaving the garage, Danny pulled out his cell and stabbed the numbers harder than necessary. Someone on the other end answered, and Danny said, "We gotta talk."

☆

As Nathaniel and Charlie arrived at the office, Sam and Terry discussed lunch.

"Great timing, guys. How about lunch—the four of us? I got to know Charlie pretty well on the tour yesterday, but I don't know the first thing about you two."

"That's a great idea, Sam. How about the cafeteria?"

"Boy, that sounds appetizing," said Terry.

"That's where your coffee came from yesterday, Terry. And I can vouch for the stir-fry."

"Ok, let's go. I'm starved," said Nathaniel. He hadn't thought about food until Sam mentioned lunch, but now his stomach was rumbling.

Charlie got his usual sandwich and secured a table by the window. The other three wandered over. Terry had a Greek salad, Sam a falafel wrap, and Nathaniel had turkey, stuffing, and green beans.

"Thanksgiving dinner? That's the most Massachusetts thing I've ever seen, Sport."

Nathaniel grinned. "I can't resist! It's in my blood."

"Don't tell me your ancestors came over on the Mayflower," said Terry.

"Not quite, but they've been in Massachusetts for a long time."

"Ok, what's everyone's favorite Thanksgiving side?" asked Sam.

"Stuffing, hands down," answered Nathaniel. "When I was a new agent, I used to eat a lot of Stovetop. Rotisserie chicken from the store, Stovetop, frozen broccoli. That's a meal." He smiled at the memory.

"Mashed potatoes and gravy for me," said Charlie. "And it's gotta be homemade—none of that canned stuff. That combination is hard to beat. My late wife always made extra gravy, so we'd have plenty for leftovers."

"I can't believe all of you have answered wrong. The answer is pie! Come on now," said Terry with a laugh. "Gotta be pie."

"What kind of pie? If you say pumpkin, I dunno if we can be friends," said Charlie.

"Charlie, I'm not a materialist. The only purpose pumpkin serves is that it's made from a vegetable, so it's easier to convince your mom to let you have it for breakfast the next morning."

"We always did that, too!" exclaimed Sam.

"But my favorite is chocolate cream with meringue, not whipped cream. My grandma always made both because I had one uncle who liked it one way and one the other. But really, I love all pie. I've got a terrible sweet tooth."

"I hate to say the same thing, but the answer is pie—Apple for me. My grandmother taught me that the best pie comes from a mix of apples. I always used to help her make the pies. We'd get up early, just the two of us in the kitchen. I have fond memories of those times."

"Well," said Charlie pushing back from the table, "I dunno about anybody else, but I'm gonna need some dessert after that." Everyone pushed back their chairs and headed towards the dessert section. There was no pie to offer, but a fresh batch of chocolate chip cookies meant no one walked away disappointed.

As they returned to the office after dessert, Nathaniel fell in step with Sam. "This lunch was an excellent idea."

Later that evening, the woods behind the Academy were dark and deep. They've long been the venue of simulated SWAT team exercises. But this evening, they were hauntingly still with the first hint of fall chill as Danny Bode's truck crunched over the gravel road behind the Academy. The road led through the woods to the picnic and recreational areas for the Marine and FBI employees and guests. At night it was pitch black, uninhabited, and quiet except for the sounds of the woods. Danny drove his tow truck slowly until he got to a sign that said "FBI Rec. Area—Authorized Personnel Only. Violators Will be Prosecuted." He turned in past the sign and drove over to the covered pavilion. His headlights shone out over the moon-bathed Lunga Reservoir, which looked gorgeous and peaceful in the moonlight. Built in the 1950s to serve Camp Barrett—the officer's training school—the reservoir was ironically named after the river on Guadalcanal where the Battle of Bloody Ridge was fought.

Three mallards landed on the water, and small animals scurried in the brush—night-woods sounds filled the crisp air. Danny saw the outline of a car parked nearer to the back of the public pavilion. He turned off his truck and got out, shivering at how much cooler it was in the woods. As he approached the pavilion, he heard a familiar voice say, "Over here, Danny." Danny walked towards the voice, but something in the underbrush darted. Danny froze. Then a small animal scurried away. Relieved, Danny walked on toward the voice.

15
LIGHTS, CAMERA, ACTION

Saturday, September 20

At 6:15 am the following day, Nathaniel stood in his black and chrome kitchen, clad in a Black Watch plaid bathrobe and LL Bean slippers, hair still wet from his shower, listening to the soothing sound of his espresso machine. He stared out the large kitchen windows that offered a sweeping view of the Potomac, thinking about the case. The sound of the Law-and-Order theme blasting from his cell phone shattered the quiet of the morning. "Shit," said Nathaniel as he picked up his phone. The FBI Director did not call him this early with good news.

"Croft."

"Please wait for the Director, Inspector."

"Nathaniel, this investigation just got worse. Danny Bode's body was discovered by an NA student running this morning. Hanging from the crane on his tow truck parked by the pavilion in the Lunga Reservoir recreation area. There's a suicide note, but I'm unconvinced."

"Two bodies in a week. This is going to cut down on outdoor runners at the Academy."

"Nathaniel, I'm in no mood for jokes this morning. The press is already circling. Button this up. I do not want another body, is that understood?"

"Yes, ma'am," said Nathaniel, but the director was already gone. He quickly thumbed Charlie's number, grabbed his coffee in the other hand, and headed to his bedroom. He put the phone on speaker and set it on his dresser.

"Do you have any idea what fucking time it is?"

"Good morning to you, too," said Nathaniel, pulling a pair of charcoal pants from his closet without looking. "Get dressed and get yourself some coffee. We got another body."

"What?! Fuck. Who?"

"Danny Bode."

"Where??"

"Hanging from the crane of his tow truck by the Lunga Reservoir pavilion. The Director called me herself."

"Oh, hell. Ok, give me half an hour. I'll meet you there. You gonna call the other two?"

"Yup," said Nathaniel, buttoning a blue shirt the same color as his eyes. His free time was next to nil, and he wouldn't spend it tidying up. He paid for a high-end cleaning service to keep his condo spotless and a laundry service to keep him in clean clothes, which some unknown person arranged according to color. He grabbed the matching tie from the hanger and brushed his teeth. Five minutes later, he was in the elevator heading to the garage, coffee still in hand. Once his BMW cleared the garage, he called Terry.

"Terry Jamison."

"Terry, it's Nathaniel. We've got another body at the Academy." Nathaniel quickly filled Terry in on the details. "Charlie and I are headed to the crime scene. I'm about to call Sam. What do you want to do?"

"I don't have any crime scene experience, so I'll head straight to the office and start pulling background on Bode. Phone records, bank statements, etc. I'll have to skip my usual breakfast in the cafeteria for visibility. You want me to call Sam?"

"Nah, I'm in the car. See you at the office later."

Nathaniel dialed Sam's number, but the call went to voicemail. "You've reached Captain Samantha Melton. Please leave a message."

"Sam, it's Nathaniel. Another body was discovered at the Academy, a guy Charlie and I talked to yesterday. We're headed to the crime scene now. Call me when you get this."

He reached into his glovebox at a stop light and pulled out a protein bar. It wasn't exactly the breakfast of champions, but his body needed fuel for what was sure to be a long day ahead. As his car hummed along the highway, Nathaniel briefly examined the prickle of disappointment he'd felt when Sam didn't pick up—before filing it away.

Twenty years as an agent had honed the compartmentalization he'd practiced since his mother's death when he was 10. He kept his mental landscape as clutter-free as he kept his condo, though he couldn't outsource the mental tidying up to a cleaning service the way he did for his home.

Ten minutes later, his phone rang. It was Sam. "Sorry, I was on my morning run. I never take my phone."

"It's your thinking time. I get it."

"Um, yeah."

"I never take my phone when I row. Plus, there's no room in a scull. But listen, I called because another body was discovered at the Academy. The Director called me herself." He heard Sam's sharp intake of breath. "Charlie and I are heading to the crime scene. Terry is going straight to the office. What do you want to do?"

"I'll join Terry. I'm sure there'll be a lot of background to wade through."

"Right. I don't think Charlie and I will stay long; I'm sure the place is swarming. We'll debrief when we arrive."

"Copy that. See you soon."

"Oh, Sam? Bring a change of civilian clothes. You have a suit?"

"Uh, sure."

"I'll explain when I see you."

As soon as she hung up with Nathaniel, Sam called Marge.

"Marge, change of plans. We caught another body. The Smithsonian will have to wait."

"Oh no. I'm sorry, Sam."

"Me too! Sorry to leave you without plans at the last minute."

"Nah, that's ok. I'll go to work and look super virtuous. Always plenty to do."

"Drink after work? I think I'll need it."

"Say the word, and Jack and I will be there."

When Nathaniel and Charlie pulled up, the reservoir was anything but tranquil. They showed their credentials and got past the FBI Agents, the security guards, the MPs, and the local cops. Finally, they made it to the inner perimeter, where they met the ranking uniform officer on the case, an MP named Martinez.

"Hey, Sergeant. What do you have?"

"Got a white male, identified as Danny Bode. Hung from the back of his tow truck crane—possible suicide. There was a note, but that doesn't necessarily mean anything. Dead maybe 7–8 hours."

Charlie said, "Damn."

"We'll share our findings with your team as soon as we have them. But you're gonna want to look at the note. Relates to your case."

Nathaniel and Charlie exchanged a look. Martinez walked them over to an NCIS crime scene tech.

"Hey Mack, can you show these agents the note?"

"Sure thing." He handed them an evidence bag.

"Mind if I take a photo?" asked Nathaniel.

"Go ahead. Then I have to lock it up."

Nathaniel set the bag down on top of an equipment case. "Charlie, stand here and give me a shadow, so there's no reflection."

"You got it, Sport."

Nathaniel snapped some photos, then held the bag so he and Charlie could read it. The note was typed on plain computer paper in Word's default sans-serif font.

I'm eternally sorry. I can't live with what I've done. I killed Rasheed. I'll be watching over you and the kids. Goodbye.

"Huh," said Nathaniel.

"Yeah, now you see why I said 'possible suicide,'" said Martinez. "You want to see the body?"

"Yes, thanks. Then we'll get out of your hair." Nathaniel and Charlie followed the MP down the path to the other side of the pavilion where the truck was. Martinez handed Nathaniel and Charlie some paper crime scene booties and held the yellow "Police Line Do Not Cross" tape. The body hanging from the tow arm looked grisly and sad in the bright morning light. Charlie and Nathaniel had both seen a fair amount of death in their line of work, but as Charlie had said to Nathaniel many years ago,

"The first time it doesn't affect you is when you should turn in your badge."

"Christ, I'm not gonna miss this shit," muttered Charlie as he walked around the corpse, taking some reference photos. But Nathaniel's focus was on the truck.

"Martinez, is it possible to move the tow arm remotely?"

Martinez smiled. "Yeah, you spotted that too, huh? We're checking with the manufacturer, but I doubt it. My uncle runs a garage, and I worked summers there in high school. Never seen a rig that did that before."

"Well, keep me posted. Charlie, you good?"

"Yep."

They walked back outside the yellow tape barrier, shedding their booties.

"Martinez, thanks for showing us around. I know you're busy, so we'll let you get to it." He held out his hand, and the two shook.

"My pleasure, Inspector. I'll send the crime scene photos and the autopsy as soon as we get them."

As they returned to the outer perimeter, Charlie asked, "What about the tow arm?"

"To get himself attached to the hook, he'd need to lower the tow arm. But then, how will he get it off the ground once he's on there? The switch is usually on the cab. It's a safety thing, so no one brains themselves accidentally."

"So he had help. The note shows premeditation, but that kind of sloppiness says shit planning."

"I agree. I'd say it wasn't meditated for very long."

As they crossed the parking lot back towards their building, they passed numerous reporters doing stand-ups. An FBI public information officer did her best to keep order until it was time to brief them.

"This morning Danny Bode, an FBI mechanic, was found dead in an apparent suicide. Speculation runs deep that he might have killed Detroit detective and National Academy student Mohammed Rasheed, who was found lynched in this same area last week. We'll update you as we get more information. Now back to you, Claudia."

Nathaniel and Charlie returned to the office and quickly debriefed Sam and Terry. Nathaniel showed them the alleged suicide note. "I know you guys have been busy here, and I want to hear about it. But Sam and I have an appointment. Put your civvies on, Captain."

Sam grabbed the garment bag hanging off her cube and disappeared to the bathroom, returning a few minutes later in a sober navy suit.

"Ready?"

"My mother told me not to go anywhere with strange men," said Sam with a smile.

"I'm wounded! We've known each other for a whole week. We're going to the Behavioral Sciences Unit. It's time we had a profile before the body count gets higher. And my favorite profiler gets squirrely around uniforms."

"Must be tough for him to work at Quantico then," said Sam as they headed for the elevator.

"It would be if he ever left the basement," said Nathaniel as he swiped his ID and hit B3.

Nathaniel and Sam got off the elevator and walked through a labyrinth of hallways three levels below the main floor of the Academy. It was like descending to the catacombs of Rome as they followed the signs for the Behavioral Sciences Unit (BSU). Sam snuck a look at Nathaniel as they walked down a drab hallway and again marveled at how well he wore his clothes. He looked like a GQ model.

Sam wished she'd had her off-the-rack suit tailored. She saw Nathaniel shoot his cuffs and laughed.

"Were you born in an Armani store?"

"Pretty sure it was Mass General. I have an uncle in the business. He had a men's shop on Milk Street in Boston. But years of rowing means my torso is an upside-down triangle. If I don't get custom-made suits, I look like a mob enforcer sent to break thumbs. If you're interested, I can give you the name of my tailor."

"I might take you up on that. Will he be offended if I ask him to fix a Banana Republic blazer?" Nathaniel smiled. Then they saw a sign that read: "BSU, John Galtz, Ph.D. Unit Chief." As they walked in, they spotted John—a mid-50s, wiry-haired, salt and pepper fossil in a rumpled shirt and slacks, loosened tie with a couple of coffee stains, dark glasses—poring over one of a half-dozen stacks on his desk. The office was dark, littered with commendations, plaques, and gifts. Some were hung up; others were stacked on top of outdated furniture. The awards were from police departments, both foreign and domestic. John didn't look up. He was engrossed as he flipped through a stack of gruesome photos of a woman who'd been raped, killed, and set on fire, sent in from a police department in the Midwest.

Nathaniel looked at Sam, smiled, and coughed. First, politely, then louder and raspier.

Without looking up, John said, "Christ, Nathaniel, you better get that cough looked at." Then, he stood up, looked up over his glasses, smiled, and reached out his right hand.

"John, this is Captain Samantha "Sam" Melton from NCIS. She's on the taskforce representing the Marine Corps." Nathaniel shook hands with John and then gave him the file jacket about two inches thick.

John looked, smiled, and nodded at Sam. He shook her hand almost shyly as he grabbed for the file. He returned to his desk and immediately started to flip through it. Nathaniel looked around. Every office space was covered with books, papers, or memorabilia. He cleared off a couple of chairs for him and Sam as she shrugged her shoulders and stifled a laugh. They watched a master at work as he sifted through the file like he was panning for gold.

Sam looked at one of the office corners. John's degrees hung there crudely and off-center—like John. They were from Virginia, Yale, and Harvard, where he'd gotten his Ph.D. in clinical psychology. Suddenly, John pushed up his glasses onto his thinning hair, looked up, and started lecturing machine-gun-style like a tenured professor who has taught this course many times.

"In the Rasheed case, they're amateurs at premeditated murder but no strangers to killing. Maybe hunters, the way they cut. By the footprints, one guy's about 6'4", another about 6' or 6'2", and a third, maybe 5'10". The short guy was in charge—you can tell by the footprint pattern. Suggests some hierarchy. Organized type. Neat, thorough, vengeful, with the bat and all." John stretched and took a sip of cold coffee, then continued, "The three could be white or Black, but all three were the same race—no integration when it comes to this kind of stuff. By the way, swastika on Rasheed was a ruse. Nazis are much more precise when they carve a swastika. Damn shame about the swastika."

Nathan said, "A shame? In what way, other than it had to hurt like hell?"

John looked up, "No, it was postmortem. Not a lot of blood. I meant a shame that the symbol of the swastika comes from Sanskrit and means 'conductive to well-being.' In fact, in many religions, like Hindu and Buddhism, it still means good luck. It got hijacked into a symbol of hate by the Nazis as an emblem of the Aryan race. After the holocaust and the fall of Hitler, the world associated the swastika—once a perfectly reputable symbol—as a symbol of atheism and Nazism."

Nathaniel looked at Sam, winked, and said, "Interesting, John. Never knew that."

By then, John was back on the case, dictating his findings. "Doesn't match anything in our databases. The Guys already ran them. Nope—amateurs. Nothing like the Green River Killer. Now, THAT guy was a REAL pro." John reached for his cup of cold coffee, took a sip, and hiked up his dark-rimmed glasses back onto the top of his head. "Gary Leon Ridgway—the Green River Killer. Now, he was a true serial murderer. They convicted him of 49 murders of young prostitutes on the West Coast. However, the estimate on the total kills was 71. A bible thumper by day and serial murder by night."

Nathaniel looked at him and said, "Again, fascinating, but how about this case, John?"

John awakened from a trance, snapped his glasses back on, and looked at the file.

"Saw the bit about green fabric under the victim's fingernails. I seriously doubt it's an NA student. Too easy to get the shirts from the PX. My guess, forensics will find that the shirts have never been washed. Have the lab test them for detergent."

Then John flipped to the second section of the file, separated by a red divider.

"This supposed suicide, Danny's, is pure bullshit—that's its technical, forensic name!" He laughed at his joke, as did Nathaniel and Sam.

"We thought so but are trying to put the pieces together."

"First, most, if not all, suicide notes are written. Think about it. The most intimate thing you can do, and you use a computer to type it out in Microsoft Word? Nah. Lotta people don't even have printers anymore."

Nathaniel nodded in agreement.

"And the note itself is more sophisticated than Danny. Listen," John said as he read aloud: "'I'm eternally sorry. I can't live with what I've done. I killed Rasheed. I'll be watching over you and the kids. Goodbye. ' Not to mention it's impersonal. He doesn't name his wife or kids. Look, I knew Danny well. He fixed my car on the side. Have to admit, I never gave it a thought that he was using Bureau parts. Nonetheless, 'eternally sorry' is just not in his vocabulary."

"Pretty much what we thought. It would have been impossible for Danny to get up on the tow arm and then elevate it to hang himself."

John paused for another hit of coffee. "What did I tell you? Amateurs. That's it for now. Let me think about it for a while. I'll call you later. Send me an e-mail if you get anything else—especially about the rope."

"To compare the two?"

"Yes. But also to see the type used. My guess, by the looks of photos, it was a quarter-inch hemp-natural fiber. Often used in Kinbaku."

"Kinbaku?" asked Nathaniel.

"Kinbaku—the art of erotic bondage—Japanese bondage rope. Nathaniel, you, of all people, should know about bondage!" Sam looked at Nathaniel, who blushed. She tucked that little nugget away for further thought.

"What do you think, John? Same killers?"

"Definitely. And they had less time to plan this one. Whatever you've discovered, it's making them nervous. This means they're getting not only sloppy but also desperate. That makes them more dangerous."

"That's good to know."

John stood up and said with a wave, "Off you go. I've got work to do. Can I keep the file for a few hours?"

"Sure. Talk to you later."

John pulled down his glasses and leafed through the file, ignoring them—discussion over. Nathaniel knew the drill with John. He looked at Sam and tilted his head towards the door. They stood and started to head out.

"Thanks, John."

"Sure. Just fix the furniture before you go."

Nathaniel and Sam dutifully put stacks back on the chairs they'd cleared to sit. As they turned down the hallway, Nathaniel heard John say, "Very interesting."

That afternoon at the daily meeting, Sam and Nathaniel filled Terry and Charlie in on what John had told them.

"I'm glad the perps think we're getting close because we've got no F'ing idea who did it," said Charlie when they'd finished.

Terry looked thoughtful. "Well, that's not entirely true. If John doesn't think it's NA students, who does that leave? FBI, NA, or Marine staff. I hate to say it, but we're looking at one of our own here."

Silence met this pronouncement.

"Well, shit," said Charlie.

"I think you're right, Terry. Which means we need to be extra careful. From now on, I want all of us to stay on campus in the FBI dorms. We're stepping up this investigation and don't have time for a commute. And we're locking up everything."

"I assume the BOQ is close enough—unless the FBI dorms have a mini fridge. Then, I'm moving."

"You don't even have a fridge? Thank you for your sacrifice," said Terry solemnly. Sam rolled her eyes.

"Ok, now you know what Sam and I have been up to. Charlie and Terry?"

"I've been going through Bode's background," said Terry as he moved a blue post-it to the "done" column. "And the more I looked at it, the more unlikely it seemed that he'd end up working for the FBI. His family's been in the same part of North Carolina since before the Civil War, and you might say they took that loss hard. They've been flying that dumbass stars and bars ever since. Some family members are known or suspected KKK or other white supremacist groups. He had some brushes with the law when he was a juvenile, though he never did time as an adult, and his juvie record is sealed. But he didn't graduate high school. Got his GED and apprenticed at a local garage. So how the hell did he end up here?"

"And how the hell did he pass an FBI background check?" asked Nathaniel.

"I had the same question, and I think the only way he does it is with help. There's nothing there that would disqualify him, necessarily, but taken together, it's pretty questionable. So my working theory is that he had help from the FBI or the Marines. But if that's true, I don't want to tip our hand by pulling his personnel file."

"Terry, this is great work. I agree about his file. So, what's your next step?"

"I want to go down to North Carolina and poke around. But since I've been following your request to be visible on campus, I think my absence will be conspicuous. So I guess my firm will have an urgent case that I have to deal with. I shouldn't need more than a few days to poke around."

"Great. How do we tell the rumor mill about this urgent matter you must deal with?"

"That part's easy," said Charlie. "We'll have a team beer tonight in the Boardroom, and Terry will get his urgent call there. You up for a little stagecraft, Terry?"

"I think I can handle that. I'll have my assistant call me. The Boardroom should be busy around 6:30, right?"

"That should do it."

"I'm guessing this is not an actual boardroom?" asked Sam.

"Nah, it's the name of the FBI bar. The wisdom of putting a bar in the middle of a federal facility cannot go understated. The closest bar is 9 miles away in Stafford. The road is dark, winding, and narrow—what could go wrong? The Boardroom keeps idiots from jeopardizing their careers by drinking and driving," explained Charlie.

"Yeah, instead of a winding road, all you have to do is find the right dorm room. A guy in my class climbed into the wrong bed after a night in the Boardroom. Never lived it down," said Terry with a laugh.

"Well, they DO all look the same," laughed Charlie.

"Oh, before I forget, I got the digital Kanban board. Before we go to the Boardroom, let's move from analog to digital," said Nathaniel, gesturing towards the post-its.

"Charlie?" asked Nathaniel, but Charlie was staring at the Kanban board. "CHARLIE."

"Jesus, Nathaniel, I do have hearing aids. But I was thinking: it's been a couple of days since our snoop has been through here. If we switch to the digital one anyway, why don't we leave the paper one up with incorrect info?"

"Classic misdirection. I think that's a great idea," said Sam. "Why don't I add a post-it that says 'Bode Marine connection?' to my 'to do' section?"

"Are you sure, Sam? If it is a Marine, that puts you in the firing line."

"I appreciate the concern, Nathaniel, but we need to know

if there's a Marine connection. Plus, I have been shot at before. Quite a few times."

Charlie watched this exchange with interest.

After Nathaniel had explained the electronic Kanban and they'd shredded any sensitive post-its, Charlie looked at his watch. "Oh look, it's time for beer and amateur theatrics."

"Who are you calling an amateur? Bet you didn't know I was a theatre minor at Howard."

"Terry! You're kidding," said Sam as she gathered up her things.

"Nope. My Iago in Othello was very well received. And it turns out that my theatre minor taught me more about being a trial lawyer than anything I learned in law school."

"Now, that I can believe."

"Ok, everyone locked up the important stuff? I'm coming back after, but I don't want to take any chances," said Nathaniel

As they filed out and Nathaniel locked the door, Sam said, "Do you need the rest of us to return? I promised to help my friend Marge set up her Hinge profile tonight. But I can come back after that."

"You understand any of that?" Charlie asked Terry.

"Nope."

"Then lets you and I go get a table and let those two figure out if they're flirting." Terry's eyebrows shot up, then he grinned.

"No need to come back," said Nathaniel. "I'll call you if anything comes up. Hinge, eh? That your weapon of choice?"

"I mean, they're all horrible. But I like the different prompts on Hinge."

"Never figured you for a dating-app person."

"Are you kidding? I don't date Marines, so where else would I ever meet someone?"

"Fair point."

Sam gave him an appraising look. "Bet you're a play-the-field man, Mr. Kinbaku."

"Don't believe everything John tells you."

"Hmm, disappointing."

Nathaniel grinned.

"Nathaniel, how old is Charlie?"

"He's 55. Why? You got a thing for sarcastic widowers?"

Sam rolled her eyes. "No, but my friend Marge… I think I have an idea. She needs a good man after her shithead ex-husband, and Charlie needs to be reminded that he's not 100 years old."

"Matchmaking! I like it. You taking new clients?"

"You need help finding a date?"

"Well, I have been busy this week. Nah, I had a casual thing in LA. Lotta fun, but that was all. What about you?"

"I've only been back in the country a few weeks. I ended a serious relationship before I left, but nothing since."

Something in her tone told Nathaniel not to pry. "Well, here we are, the legendary Boardroom. You ready for the show?"

"Absolutely."

The bar was busy but not packed. Charlie and Terry had found a table near the middle of the bar, in an ideal location to be overheard.

"First round's on me. What's everybody drinking?" asked Nathaniel.

"Whatever's on draft. And none of that IPA garbage," said Charlie.

"Glass of red, please. Cabernet if they have it," said Terry.

"Gin and tonic, two limes. You need help carrying four drinks?"

"Uh, probably," said Nathaniel sheepishly.

"All they teach you in the FBI, and you can only carry one drink in each hand?"

Nathaniel grinned and shrugged. When the drinks appeared

on the bar, Sam expertly gathered the two pints of beer into one hand and picked up her G&T with the other. "Think you can handle Terry's wine?"

"And what part of basic training is that?"

"The kind you get as a waitress. That was my summer job all through high school," said Sam as she delivered the drinks.

"Cheers," said Nathaniel, and everyone toasted.

"Bet this one never had a summer job," said Charlie, gesturing with his beer toward Nathaniel.

"I did! I taught sailing in Marblehead."

The other three burst out laughing. "Sport, if that was meant to make you sound like a man of the people, it failed."

Nathaniel blushed.

"What about you, Terry?" asked Nathaniel.

"What didn't I do? I was a lifeguard. I've done every job in a restaurant except chef. And you're looking at the Fairlawn Gap Employee of the Month for July 1992." He straightened the lapels on his suit as he said this, and everyone laughed.

"Oh, I hope that certificate is framed in your office," said Sam.

"Right under my law degree, naturally. Charlie? What'd you do?"

"I was a camp counselor." Roars of laughter met this announcement.

"What! You never told me that," laughed Nathaniel.

"Why is that so funny? I'm great with kids!" retorted Charlie, but he was grinning.

"What kind of camp?" asked Sam, wiping tears of laughter.

"YMCA. It was fun. All outdoors, tons of activities. And it beat the shit out of picking strawberries on my uncle's farm, which was my other option."

The group had such a good time that no one noticed Terry's vibrating phone until it bumped Charlie's pint glass and made a shrill noise. Terry put the phone to his ear.

"Hi, Kate. What's—the judge said what?" Terry roared. "And what did Patterson say? Shit. Ok. I'm on my way. No one does anything else until I get there. Is that clear? Is that clear?? Good." Terry stood. "Nathaniel, I'm sorry—emergency at the firm. I may be gone for a couple of days. I hate to leave you short-staffed."

"No problem at all, Terry. I understand." Nathaniel stood, and the two shook. Terry grabbed his coat and strode towards the door. All around them, bar patrons were trying to watch the drama without being obvious. Most were failing.

"Well, shit," said Charlie.

"Yup. Let's get back to the office," said Nathaniel, finishing his pint. "I need to call the Director."

As they left, conversations resumed, but a few eyes followed them out. Tucked into one of the corner booths, Ralph Pelham's deputy Jack Eller picked up his phone and sent a rapid-fire series of texts.

As Nathaniel, Sam, and Charlie crossed the darkened lawn back toward their building, Charlie said quietly, "Well, I bet his Iago was pretty good."

Sam stopped at her room to change into regulation green sweats and a Marines hoodie and grab a bottle of bourbon from her closet. Then she went down the hall and knocked on Marge's door. "You ready?" asked Sam with a grin.

"I'm gonna need some of that first," said Marge, gesturing to the bourbon. "I can't believe I'm about to make a profile on a dating app."

"You'll be fine! Besides, making the profile isn't hard. It's wading through the idiots that come after."

"Is that supposed to make me feel better?"

"Yes?" They both laughed. Marge got two glasses from her bathroom and splashed bourbon and water into each.

"Ok, let's start by finding photos you like of yourself." Marge groaned and took a large sip of bourbon.

"Eyes on the prize: a non-single bed." The two sat side by side on Marge's single bed, hunched over her phone.

"Ok, looking for?"

"Non-cheating, non-dirtbag?"

"How about the age range? 35–55?"

"I'm not dating someone ten years younger!"

"Why not? Men do it all the time."

"You know what? You're right. Fine."

"Non-smoker, no drugs?"

"But must drink," said Marge, taking a sip of bourbon. "I need a snack." She opened her desk drawer and pulled out a bag of Cool Ranch Doritos. "Want some?"

"OMG, I haven't had these since high school! I'm using that for your 'two truths and a false' prompt."

In no time, they'd crafted Marge a profile and put a serious dent in the bottle of bourbon.

"It's done! You live on Hinge," said Sam, handing the phone back to Marge.

"Cheers to that," said Marge as they clinked glasses. "Seriously, Sam, thanks for the help. I would have second-guessed myself on every part."

"Happy to help! I had a girlfriend help me with mine, too."

"Have you restarted yours since you've been back stateside?"

"I did, but I haven't looked much. I haven't had time! Plus, here I swear to secrecy, the lead agent on the task force is…hot. But, also technically, my boss! Ugh."

"Well, the task force won't last forever. And this doesn't break your no-Marines rule. Just sayin'! What's he like?"

"Former Stanford rower. A blue-blood from Massachusetts, definitely posh. You should see his car. But a natural leader. And a good team player."

"Sounds good to me. So, hurry up and solve this thing already!" They drank in companionable silence for a few minutes.

"Marge, can I ask you something?"

"Sure thing."

"You remember that speeding ticket I got that I thought was bogus? Well, Wilson asked me to come in tomorrow to talk about it. And I have the strangest feeling that he will make it disappear but expects information in return. Like he manufactured this whole thing to have a hold on me. Does that sound like him? Or is working with spies making me paranoid?"

"You're not paranoid. That sounds like him. Transactional is his middle name. And he's devoted to General Mathers. Devoted. They've served together for a long time. I understand that Wilson will do anything to ensure this confirmation goes through. Be careful with him."

"That's, unfortunately, confirming the sense I got. I'm a Marine and happy to report on anything related to the Corps. But the fact that he felt like he needed to have something on me makes me wonder what he has to hide."

"I wish I knew. But my guess is that man's got a closet full of skeletons. As my Gran would say, he gives me the shivers."

"Oh shit, look at the time. I've got to get to bed. We can go through your matches tomorrow night!"

"Oh lord. Thanks again, Sam!" They hugged goodbye, and Sam walked down the hall to her room, embarrassed to have her suspicions confirmed. She'd have to talk to Nathaniel before seeing Wilson tomorrow. Perhaps it was the bourbon or the Doritos, but the thought made her smile.

16
RECONNECTING

Sunday, September 21

At 8 am the following day, Nathaniel, Charlie, and Sam arrived at the office. Sam made a beeline for the coffee machine, Nathaniel unlocked the safe, and Charlie checked his security alarms. His dictionary was still pointing due north, but when he fired up his computer, there was an alert that the motion sensor camera had picked up something overnight.

"Hey guys, we got one." Sam and Nathaniel came over, and Charlie ran the footage. It was low-quality black and white, but the image of a person rifling through the desks was unmistakable.

"Is that… I almost don't want to say," said Nathaniel.

"Jack Eller? Yeah, it looks like it to me. I got no problem saying it."

"Well, shit."

"Guys, fill me in. Who is Jack Eller?"

"He's Pelham's deputy," said Nathaniel.

"Oh shit."

"Ok, we need to confirm this. Let's take it to the Academy's lab and see if they can clean it up. We can walk it over on a thumb drive. Keep it between us."

"Good idea, Sport. Let me call over and see if they're also working on a Sunday." Charlie reached for the phone.

"Before you go, can I talk to you about Wilson? Sam asked.

"Of course. Can we talk while I make coffee? I slept in the FBI dorm last night and missed my espresso machine this morning."

"Mmm, I wouldn't know anything about dorm living." Nathaniel had the good grace to look embarrassed.

"You remember my speeding ticket? The more I thought about it, the more it seemed fishy. It wasn't even close to what I was driving, and it conveniently put me into the reckless driving category, a court martial offense. He will offer to make it disappear, giving him leverage on me. So last night, I talked with my friend Marge, who has been assigned to help prepare the general for his confirmation. And she confirmed that that's very much Wilson's MO. She told me he's fiercely loyal to the general and sees most interactions with others as transactional. Now, he could just be hedging his bets. Or he could have something to hide. So how do you want to play this?"

Nathaniel studied her for a moment. "I think you have an idea. Tell me."

"I'd like to talk to him and hint that we have a suspect and that Terry left because the suspect is Black. I noticed the other day that there are no Black staffers in the general's office. Given the racial makeup of the Corp, that's hard to do by accident. If Wilson is involved, that should put him at ease. If he's not, we're not giving him any information."

"That's a fantastic idea. Does the Marine Corps specialize in counter-intelligence at the EWS?"

"That's need-to-know, I'm afraid," said Sam with a wink.

Charlie came up to them. "Ok, I got a tech on the phone at the digital lab. He's semi-willing to have something interesting to do. You ready?"

"Great, let's go. You going to see Wilson now?"

"I was, but now I'm wondering if I shouldn't stay here until you return. Should we keep someone in the office until we sort out the intruder?"

Nathaniel considered a moment. "They'd have to be brazened to try something during the day, even on a Sunday. Let's be vigilant about locking the door and keeping sensitive papers in the safe. I don't want to tip our hand by suddenly being on guard. "

"Copy that. Ok, see you back here later then."

A few minutes later, Charlie and Nathaniel stood in the FBI Academy's digital lab, mainly used for training and development and rarely for investigations. A skinny guy in a hoodie looked up from his screen as they walked in. "Can I help you?" he asked in a voice that suggested he didn't want to.

"Are you Kevin? I'm Charlie. We spoke on the phone earlier."

"Oh! Right! You need some footage cleaned up. Come on over here." This challenge excited the otherwise bored technician, who had sprung into action. He led Charlie and Nathaniel to a sizeable double monitor set up and plugged in the thumb drive Nathaniel handed him. He viewed the grainy video as he hit buttons to enhance the image. The picture got better, then worse, then better. He hit the final button and leaned back. A progress bar that said "Rendering" appeared on the screen. Finally, he pointed at an image that had been cleared up enough to make it identifiable. Nathaniel and Charlie stared at the image as Charlie said, "Holy shit, it is Jack Eller!"

"Should I know who that is?" asked Kevin.

"No, and I'd appreciate it if you didn't mention this little project to anyone," said Nathaniel.

"What project?" said Kevin as he handed over the thumb drive with the enhanced image.

"Attaboy, Sport."

"Thanks again, Kevin."

Kevin waved as he strolled back to his counter. Nathaniel heard what sounded suspiciously like the Star Trek theme song as they walked back down the hall.

☆

It was a bright morning on the Quantico Marine Corps golf course. Established in 1930 as The Officers' Golf Club, the original Course had only six holes. In the 1940s, the Course was expanded to 18 holes, as finely manicured as a Marine haircut, and renamed the Quantico Golf Course. And in 1980, the Course was renamed the Medal of Honor Golf Course in honor of the Corps' mega-heroes. Over the years, the Course became a trendy, quick getaway for Presidents of the United States who liked to play golf, including Nixon, Ford, Bush, Clinton, and Trump.

Just after 9 am that morning, many crew cuts in various groups were already whacking the tiny white ball around. On the second green stood Avery Wilson in spiffy golf attire: grey pants, a blue polo, and black and white shoes, with a white leather glove on his left hand. Sam approached the green from the footpath for golf carts, watching as Wilson sunk a 20-footer.

"Pretty impressive, Sergeant Major," Sam said.

Wilson tipped his visor and walked over, leaving the other foursome to putt out their balls.

"So, Captain, what's new?"

"I think we're zeroing in on a suspect."

"And I heard it might be a Marine suspected of the deed," Wilson said.

"I can't say anything about that, sir. But you heard Terry Jamieson quit?"

That brought the sergeant major up short. "I heard he had to go back to his law firm."

"Well, that's what the FBI Director wants everyone to think. It's not a great look for the only Black task force member to quit. But it was just after we first started looking hard at this suspect. Now, why do you think that would be?"

Wilson smiled. "That's very interesting, Captain. I can see you were the right choice for this task force."

"Thank you."

One of the other golfers waved to Wilson, and he returned to his golf cart. "Well, please keep in touch, Captain. The General's hearin's on the 29th—just over a week."

"Of course," she said as she turned and walked off.

Sam could feel Wilson's eyes on her ass as she walked away. She suppressed the urge to shiver. "Every time I talk to that guy, I feel like I need a shower," she thought as she returned to her car.

After the golf course, Sam thought she'd try her luck on Rasheed's file again. She entered the Marine Corps Base Quantico Provost Marshall's (PMO) Office. The Marine Corps equivalent of a police station, the PMO's layout was expansive. On a large wall to the right of the reception area, a plaque bearing the Mission Statement held pride of place:

> MISSION: Continually, the Marine Corps Base Quantico Provost Marshal Office protects the lives, rights, and property of all personnel and organizations aboard the installation to support unit and personnel readiness and create and preserve an atmosphere of safety and security.

It looked like a police station, only in Marine green rather than police blue. A dispatcher in the corner was talking on the radio to patrol cars in service, desks with files and computers, a counter, wanted posters, and a log book. A tall Marine Corporal met Sam at the reception desk. His nametag said, "Corporal Wilson."

"Morning, Corporal. I need to talk to Gunny Romney." She

looked at the young Marine's nametag again. "Hey, Corporal, any relation to Sgt. Major Wilson?"

"Yes, Ma'am, he's my father."

She nodded. "What are the odds that Wilson's son would end up here at Quantico and as an MP? That's a pretty plum assignment," she thought to herself.

In strutted a massive Marine, shaved head, broad shoulders, barrel-chested, and sporting the nametag Romney. Confident, cocky, and quite a presence, when Romney saw Sam's rank, he took the toothpick out of his mouth, broke it in two, and tossed it into the trash. "Hello, Captain. How can I help you?"

"Gunny, I'm with NCIS assigned to the FBI Taskforce at the FBI Academy. I put a trace on a personnel file for Mohammed Rasheed. The St. Louis Military Records Facility showed that it was checked out to Quantico's Provost's Office. Can you locate that file for me?"

Without even thinking about it, he answered, "No, Ma'am. We don't have that file."

"Who does, then?"

"Don't know, ma'am."

She showed him the official tracking document.

He glanced at it and said, "Nope. Not here."

Sam scowled, "Well, Gunny, could you at least check around a little first before you tell me it's not here?"

He put his hands on his hips and puffed out his chest, "Captain, I know what's in my shop. So, I don't have to check around. Ma'am," he added as an afterthought.

"Well, thanks for all your help," she said, her voice dripping in sarcasm. "If that file surfaces, please let me know ASAP." As she walked out, she turned toward Corporal Wilson. "Nice to meet you, Corporal."

"Thank you, Ma'am. Have a nice day."

Romney returned to his office, pulled out his cell phone, dialed, and waited.

☆

When Sam returned to the office, Nathaniel and Charlie were at their desks. "How'd it go at the lab?"

"It's Eller. Clear as a bell," Nathaniel said, coming out of his office. "Did Wilson swallow your story?"

"Hook, line, and sinker. It'll be interesting to see who that rumor spreads to. I stopped into the PM's office to see about Rasheed's file. The gunny swore to me that the file wasn't there, even though he didn't even look, but the tracking document showed that's where it was. I'm convinced there's something in there that someone doesn't want us to see."

"I agree. We've got to figure out what that is. Sam, can you track down some guys who served with Rasheed?"

"Absolutely. I'll jump right on that. I did learn something interesting: Wilson's son is an MP at Quantico. He was stationed at the front desk."

"That seems like a very desirable posting, am I right?" asked Nathaniel.

"Extremely. That means General Mathers is as devoted to Wilson as Wilson is to him. It would take someone at his level to arrange that."

"That's very interesting. Let's proceed with caution. Everything we know so far is pointing to high-level collaboration here."

Sam and Charlie returned to their desks, and Nathaniel stared out the window, thinking about what they knew. His reverie was broken by the sound of his cell phone ringing. Not the Law-and-Order theme, for once, but the James Bond theme.

With a smile, he reached for his phone. "Hi, Terry. How's it going?"

"Still hot as a bastard down here. But I've got some info."

"Hang on. I'll get the other two." Nathaniel poked his head out of his office. "Hey guys, I've got Terry. Come in, and I'll put him on speaker."

Once they were all gathered, Nathaniel said, "Ok, Terry. Go ahead. Where are you calling from?"

"Hey, Nathaniel. I'm calling from a motel room. The finest rural North Carolina has to offer."

"Where are you exactly?"

"Who the hell knows? Everything down here is named after pine trees. But I have some good stuff."

"Shoot."

"Checked out the numbers I got from Rasheed's roommate's phone two days before Rasheed was killed. Rasheed routinely borrowed it. He was paranoid about being tracked."

"It's not paranoia—" started Charlie, and the other three finished in chorus: "If they're out to get you."

"The number is the Marine Corps' main number at the Pentagon. And the other number is the main number at Quantico's Marine Headquarters. Still trying to trace where the calls went from there. That's trickier."

"Great work. If you need me to run the traces, let me know."

"No need. Our law firm uses a great security group. Owner's an ex-CIA type."

"Not an ex-FBI type? Terry, I'm surprised at you," said Charlie in his best-disappointed dad voice.

"Hey, Charlie. You do remember I sued the FBI, right?"

Charlie chuckled.

"Have you found people who knew Danny Bode?" asked Nathaniel.

"Oh yeah, this has been a fruitful trip. Every third person I come across is related to Bode. I found an old Black farmer who remembers Danny Bode as a kid. He says he wasn't a bad kid when he was by himself. But he did have an evil buddy a couple of years older. They got into serious trouble, but Danny was only 16 and skated. The older one got a choice from the judge: go to jail or enlist in the military. He chose the Marines. Guess what his name is."

"I have a feeling it's going to be familiar."

"Sure is, Avery T. Wilson."

Stunned silence met this announcement.

"Guys?"

"Sorry, Terry, we're all a little shocked. Wilson has been giving Sam a hard time."

"That asshole. I know this complicates things for us politically."

"Not only that, but General Mathers' confirmation hearing is in less than two weeks. If Wilson is involved, it's a safe bet Mathers is too. And the closer it gets to the hearings, the more protective they will get. We have to tread extremely carefully here. And we need to find the connection between Wilson and Pelham," said Nathaniel.

"Pelham?"

"Turns out it's his deputy, Jack Eller, who has been snooping around our office. Charlie's camera caught him red-handed."

"Now that's interesting. Well, I've got a few more sources to talk to, but I think I'll be done today. I should be back in the office tomorrow. Anything else on your end I should know?"

"That's great, Terry. I implied to Wilson that you quit because we had a Black suspect to throw him off the scent, and before you come back, I need to tell him something, so he doesn't get suspicious. Sorry, I hope you don't mind."

Terry's deep laugh boomed from the phone. "You mean you used his prejudices as misdirection? I most certainly do not mind."

"Ok, Terry, good luck down there. Keep us posted, and I'll keep you in the loop on anything we discover here."

"Copy that. Jamieson out."

"Well, that's interesting," said Sam.

"Sure is. But let's discuss it over lunch, eh? I'm starved," said Charlie.

"Let's grab some sandwiches from the cafe and bring them back here," said Nathaniel. "We're on a roll. Feels like we're getting close, and I don't want to lose momentum."

☆

Freshly supplied with sandwiches, the task force buzzed with activity. Charlie, Nathaniel, and Sam worked on incoming information: Background on the key players, bank statements, phone records, and social media accounts. Charlie ensured everything was in the CaseMaster database and flagged anything interesting for the 4 pm meeting. Charlie walked into Nathaniel's office to ask him a question, but Nathaniel was deep in thought, looking out at Sam, his reading glasses perched on his head.

"Hey, Nathaniel?" Charlie asked after popping his head into Nathaniel's office.

Nathaniel roused from his trance, mumbling "Wilson and Pelham" to himself.

"OK? What's—"

"Wilson got Sam on the task force by having the Commandant call the Director."

"Yeah?"

"Normally, Wilson would have just asked his friend Pelham to put a Marine on the task force, right?"

"That's what I would've done. Take the path of least resistance."

"Or maybe he does, but Pelham, who knows me all too well, knows I'd block it."

Charlie thought and said, "So, Pelham coaches Wilson about Bureau politics and to end run you by going to the Director?"

"Bingo."

"Pelham's shrewder than I thought."

"Listen, he's a bureau politician and an Olympic-class ass-kisser around the Director. I've watched him up close and personal. But think I underestimated his talent."

"Next, we find out that Jack Eller, Pelham's Deputy, broke into our office. It looks like all roads lead to Ralph Pelham. But why?"

Nathaniel paused to sip his coffee. "He either owes Wilson, or Wilson has something on him? Only one way to find out," Nathaniel said as he reached for the phone. He dialed, then put a finger to his lips and put the phone on speaker.

"Is he in? It's Inspector Croft."

"Just a minute, Inspector."

A pause on the other end, then "Ralph Pelham."

"Ralph, Nathaniel. I need to talk to you about some peculiar things happening here. We had a break-in. Nothing serious taken, but I want to talk to you about the security of our space."

"A break-in? Should I send a duty agent and a few officers over to do a crime scene this morning?"

"No, not that serious. Tomorrow I have to drive to DC to brief the Director at 10. When I get back, I want to talk to you."

"No problem. Swing by when you get back."

"OK, see you then." Nathaniel told Charlie, "Let's see if Wilson says anything to Sam the next time they talk."

Nathaniel, Sam, and Charlie gathered for the 4 pm briefing that afternoon.

"Terry texted me his flight info, and he should be here for the 4 pm meeting. I want us all here to debrief together."

"Good idea. I'll see Danny's deputy Eddie at the garage tomorrow. He may want to chat with someone now that his boss has been murdered."

"Good idea, Charlie. I got the sense he was checking on Danny when he poked his head in while we were talking. Sam, what about you?"

"I'll talk to Wilson and let him know Terry is returning. This time, I'll imply that the Director begged him, political correctness, etc." She sighed.

"I'm not looking forward to it. Frankly, Wilson gives me the creeps."

"Is he still holding the ticket over your head?" asked Charlie.

"He hasn't mentioned it, so yes. Feels like he's waiting until I disappoint him so he can bring it up again."

"Sam, I know you can handle yourself. But be careful with Wilson. If he's as involved in this as we think, he's dangerous and an alpha asshole."

"That's for sure. Let's say I will see him during business hours when his office is full of staffers for a reason."

"It seems pretty likely that Wilson and Pelham are in something together, so we've all got to watch our backs," said Charlie.

"Oh, and Sam: I called Pelham this afternoon and told him we'd had a break-in. See if Wilson brings it up to you."

"Well, this is a cheerful way to end a meeting. Who's up for a drink in the Boardroom?" asked Charlie.

"Even the Lord rested on the seventh day," said Sam with a smile.

The Boardroom on a Sunday evening was empty, and the three grabbed a table towards the back. "The usual?" asked Nathaniel. Charlie nodded, and Sam followed him to the bar.

When they were settled in, Nathaniel asked, "Sam, what's the word on Mathers' confirmation? Is it expected to go through?"

"That's the scuttlebutt. Everyone expects him to fly through unless he's got a giant skeleton in his closet. But that seems unlikely at this point. My friend Marge is on his preparation team, and he's prepping as though it will be a fight. But I don't think even he expects that."

"So, no rumors, huh?"

"What are you getting at, Sport?"

"Well, we know he's hiding something. In my experience, the bigger the secret, the more the rumors swirl. But they seem to have this locked down very tightly."

"That's interesting. And true. But people who serve under Mathers seem devoted to him. Then again, is the staff packed with loyalists? Who else did they pull strings for—if they got Wilson's son a nice MP job at Quantico?"

"That's a good point, Sam. Can your friend Marge get us a list of everyone on his staff? I'd be interested to see how long they'd been serving with him. Just in case we need to apply some leverage."

"I'll ask. Shouldn't be too hard to come by."

Just then, Charlie's phone buzzed. "Oh Christ, it's my mother's nursing home. I gotta take this." He slid out of the booth and hurried for the exit.

"Charlie's mom's in a nursing home?"

"Yeah, back in Detroit. Her dementia is bad. She's only in her early 80s. She was quite the woman, from what Charlie says. I think that's where he got his wry sense of humor."

"That's so sad. It's an awful disease. I watched what it did to my grandmother. It's tough on the caretakers too. My mom spent so much time flying back and forth."

"Yes, it is. And after years of nursing Dianne through cancer, Charlie's done a lot of caretaking."

"Sounds like he needs someone to care for him for a while."

"You still have matchmaker ambitions?" asked Nathaniel with a grin.

"Why yes, I do."

Nathaniel's phone buzzed, and he picked it up. "Charlie says he's got something to take care of and not to expect him back tonight."

"I hope everything is ok."

"Me too. Not that he'd tell me if it wasn't."

"Well, this didn't exactly turn into a cheerful outing. Shall we get out of here? I could do with a walk."

Dusk was falling as they left the Boardroom. "You hungry?"

asked Sam, pulling on her jacket. "We could get sandwiches and do a walking picnic."

"What's a walking picnic?"

"I think it's something my dad made up to tire out his active children. But it's eating while walking and looking at the scenery."

"Sounds fun. Sandwiches from the cafe?"

Provisioned with hot coffee and sandwiches, they wandered along the well-lit walking paths of the FBI campus.

"Maybe it's a good thing Charlie didn't come with us. They were out of turkey and cheese," said Sam as she took a bite of her salami and cheese.

"True. He'd have pitched a fit," said Nathaniel unwrapping his ham and cheese with his teeth.

"Ok, this is harder than I remembered it," said Sam with a laugh. "Shall we find a bench?"

"Good idea. Otherwise, there's a solid chance I will ingest some of this plastic wrap."

They settled into the benches that bordered the large lawn in front of the Academy building, setting their coffees between them.

"So, do you have fond memories of Quantico?" asked Sam.

"Not really, if I'm honest. I made a couple of close friends, but everyone here is single-minded. It was competitive and cutthroat. I was much happier once I got out in the field."

"With Charlie."

"It's not hyperbole to say that Charlie taught me everything worth knowing about being an agent. But he also treated me like just a guy. He didn't give a shit about my background or my money. He was more of a father to me in the three years I worked for him than my actual father was in all the years before that. Charlie helped me see that making choices to spite my father wouldn't make me happy. But, I liked being an FBI agent and was good at it. If I'd had a different training agent, I might have washed out and ended up just another miserable finance guy." He paused to take a sip of coffee. "Jesus, you must be an excellent interrogator. I never talk about this stuff."

"I am. You'd be surprised how many men want a sympathetic woman's ear."

"No, that makes perfect sense to me. So, now it's your turn. How did you end up a career Marine?"

"My dad was a retired officer who taught at the Naval Post Graduate School in Monterrey, California. I grew up around plenty of active and retired officers. But I think the feeling of being part of a unit drew me to the Marines. I loved soccer and being part of the team. There wasn't a way to make that a career without moving to the UK. But if I joined the military, I could be on a team for the rest of my life. And I ended up in NCIS because I've always had an overdeveloped sense of justice and fairness. Being a lawyer didn't appeal to me but helping bring people to justice did. I could never sit in an office all day or a law library all night. But being in the field, solving crimes…well, each day is different. And if I'm candid, I like feeling like Nancy Drew."

"Who doesn't? My mother read me Nancy Drew novels when I was little. She said they were better than the Hardy Boys. She had the whole set from when she was a girl. I still have them somewhere."

"How old were you when she died?" asked Sam.

"Eleven. It was awful. My father tried to get rid of everything that was hers, and if it hadn't been for some quick thinking by my nanny, he would have. And he married his younger mistress less than a year later, which caused another scandal. I went to boarding school when I was twelve and never lived at home again. I see two much younger half-siblings once a year or so. I like my stepmother; I stopped hating her years ago. It was my father who was such a prick. It's easier now that he's dead. It sounds horrible when I say it out loud, but it's true." Nathaniel looked down and noticed Sam's hand slid into his while talking. He turned to look at her.

"It doesn't sound horrible to me," she said softly.

"Sam..." he said as he stroked her cheek. She leaned towards him, and he bent his head to kiss her. He kissed her deeply, and she kissed him back. He slid along the bench to close the space between them, but as he did so, his thigh nudged his coffee cup, splashing the remnants of cold coffee on them both. They sprang apart.

"Shit! I'm sorry," said Nathaniel as he tried to mop up the mess with a wad of napkins.

"I hope you're only apologizing for the coffee," said Sam wiping down one uniformed leg. "You have to hand it to Marine green; nothing shows."

Nathaniel stood up and pulled Sam to him. "You know, there are other benches," he said as he slid an arm around her waist.

"Nathaniel... I want to do more than you know. But you're technically my boss. We shouldn't. Not to mention I'm in uniform."

"Goddamn it, you do have an overgrown moral compass. But you're right. We'd better solve this case ASAP," he said with a grin.

"I'll say." Sam pulled him into the shadow of a maple by the bench. "But since we've already broken the rules... one for the road?" She slid her arms around his neck, bringing his face close to hers. His only answer was to pull her close.

"I hate your stupid rules," murmured Nathaniel into her neck some minutes later.

"Mmm...I didn't make them! But I'd better go home before we break them in half." She took a purposeful step backward and straightened her lapels. Nathaniel sighed and brushed down his suit jacket. Gathering up their trash, he said,

"I'll walk you home."

"Nathaniel. Are you going to give me your letterman jacket too?"

He laughed. "We're just two colleagues taking a walk and enjoying the scenery."

"Fine," said Sam with a grin.

They walked back to the BOQ at a respectable distance apart, chatting about the case.

"This is me. Will you check on Charlie when you get back?"

"Of course."

"Goodnight, Nathaniel."

"Night, Sam. See you tomorrow."

Nathaniel turned and walked back to his dorm. Sam went straight up to her floor without a backward glance. But she couldn't keep the smile off her face.

17
THE CONNECTION

Monday, September 22

The following day, Charlie interviewed Eddie Ramcheck on his turf. Eddie had been with Danny for years and knew all his contacts, at least those who entered the garage. The garage opened at 8 am, and when Charlie arrived at 8:15, it was already busy.

When Charlie entered the garage, several mechanics worked on official vehicles, from pick-up trucks to sedans. Eddie was working on a Bureau car installing a new secure radio. Sprawled out over the front seat, with his head under the dashboard and his feet on the garage floor, he worked to get the parts to fit. He looked, Charlie thought, like a jump-suited yogi.

When he looked up and saw Charlie, he jumped and said, "Shit."

"Well, hello to you too, Eddie."

"Sorry," he said, "It's been a pain in the ass. Danny's gone, I'm supposed to get stuff done, and I just lost my boss."

"And your friend."

Eddie nodded slowly.

"It was an awful thing. But I need to talk to you to clear up some issues. I'm sure you understand."

"Yeah, but not here. Too many ears," he said, looking around at the three other mechanics. "Let's go to Danny's private office."

"Sounds good to me," Charlie said as he headed to the glassed-in office with Danny's famous stripper pen.

"No, his private office, where no one can hear. Follow me." Eddie grabbed a set of car keys from Danny's middle desk drawer and left the garage. He led Charlie to the far edge of the employee parking lot, where a red 2005 Buick LaSabre sat in mint condition. He opened it, hopped in behind the wheel, and gestured to Charlie to join him on the passenger side. The interior was grey leather with wood trim on the dashboard. A large console separated the front seats. The size and feel of the seats were like sitting first class on a plane—plenty of legroom, even for Eddie.

Charlie said, "Wow, this is in great shape! My uncle used to have one of these. It felt big enough to live in when I was a kid."

"Yeah. I think Danny's dad had one too. This was the private place Danny took you to tell you inside stuff or ream you out."

"Kind of an office within an office."

"Yep."

"What else happened in here? Danny ever meet people here?"

"Nah, not that I know of, just guys from the shop. He had a lot of lunches here—gave him some peace and quiet."

"Anything else?"

"He made private phone calls from here, too."

"On his Bureau cell?"

"Nope, he used his cell."

"We never did find his cell when we searched him and his truck. Any thoughts about where it might be?"

"With whoever murdered him."

"What?"

"C'mon, who leaves a typed suicide note? Total bullshit! I have seen enough *Law and Order* to know better."

Charlie was surprised but tried to keep his face neutral. "Eddie, I'm impressed. What else do you think about the case?"

"Think Danny was a good guy but weak—got in over his head."

"Say more about that."

"Danny was a little guy, wiry, tough, but small. So, he was intimidated by big guys or guys in power."

"Like you?"

"Yeah, but Danny was a mentor to me. He hired me as a kid, just starting to break bad. Taught me a trade. Like a father to me."

"So, he followed the leader of the pack."

"Yep, that was Danny. He wasn't a bad guy, but he'd make bad decisions when he was with bad dudes."

"Like who?"

"Well, years ago, he hung out with a bunch of motorcycle guys from a local biker club. Not a bunch of outlaws, more like a group of freelance assholes. They'd get drunk, tear up a bar, ride over someone's lawn, or bust some headlights. Asshole stuff."

"So, Danny had a motorcycle?"

"Yep, a Harley. Got rid of it and his asshole friends about five years ago. For a while, he hung out at a local bar with some Marines, maybe six months or so, but stopped when he started his side business."

"Talk to me about the business."

"OPR has all that—they tore up Danny one side and down the other."

"Give me the short version, then."

"Danny wanted to send his kids to college. Never saw them much after his wife split and moved with their three kids back to West Virginia, where she's from. So, Danny wanted to make it up to the kids.

"One thing led to another, so Danny started staying after work. Never started working on outside cars until after 5 to keep things on the up and up. Always bought parts outside at an AutoJoint place and brought them in. Except for using the equipment, he never misused anything."

"So, what happened?"

"Too much success!"

"Explain."

"Word spread and Danny had more clients than he could handle. So, he asked me to help, and then a couple of the other mechanics. When we got pushed, we used leftover parts in the shop. First, a little, then a lot. In the end, Danny called it the slippery slope of success."

"Pretty insightful of old Danny."

"Yeah, we had customers who were FBI, Marines, and even civilians from the Base started coming."

"Business expanded even to the Marines?"

"Yeah, Danny knew a bunch of the Marines. He might have even known one or two guys from North Carolina, where he grew up."

"Anyone in particular you recall?"

"Just some guy he called 'T.' Pretty sure he knew Danny back home in North Carolina. T was small, wiry, and tough as hell—the way he talked and carried himself. He never wore a uniform when he came by, but you could tell he was a Marine. He only came by a few times. He mostly called over the past few months."

"How'd you know it was him calling?"

"Saw his initial T show up on Danny's cell a couple of times when Danny's phone was on his desk."

"Even after the car repair operation stopped?"

"Yes, especially in the past month or two."

"Sounds odd."

"Yeah, and Danny started taking all the calls in the car. Saw Danny taking notes in a pocket notebook. I had to come out and get him a couple of times."

"Hmm."

"Yeah, I never liked that guy T. The way Danny kowtowed to him—like he was a big shot. "

"You have any more info on T or Danny?"

"Not really, and I got to get back."

"Eddie, you've been helpful. I may need to follow up later. Thanks."

"Danny was a friend. I want to..." his voice caught, so he coughed to cover up his sudden, unexpected burst of emotion.

Sam took a deep breath and walked into Wilson's office. She got a wink from Marge as she walked by. She knocked on the doorframe of his office.

"Good morning, Captain. Come in, have a seat."

"Thank you."

"You have an update for me?"

"I do. Terry Jamieson is coming back."

"Does that mean you've moved on to another suspect?"

"No, from what I overheard, I suspect the FBI Director did some persuading. Keeping up appearances and that sort of thing. But he should be back today or tomorrow."

"And I'm sure they'll say he fixed whatever the emergency was at his firm."

"Yes."

"Captain, I heard a rumor you had a break-in. Is that true?"

"It is. Strange though—nothing was taken, just a few papers shuffled around."

"I see. Anything else you can tell me, Captain?"

"Not much. I'm digging through a lot of background, but nothing interesting yet. I'll keep you posted."

"Do that, Captain. That's all," he said as he returned to the papers on his desk.

"Thank you." Sam rose swiftly and left Wilson's office, walking briskly to the exit. She did not exhale until she was safely in her car.

☆

That afternoon Terry Jamison walked into the task force office. All decked out in his grey pin-striped-go-to-trial suit and carrying his alligator briefcase. He was greeted by a few balloons, some streamers, and a chorus of "For He's a Jolly Good Fellow." Surprised, he stopped just inside the doorway. Sam yelled, "Speech! Speech!" Nathaniel and Charlie joined in.

"Hey, good to be back. It's been interesting. I learned that I could get back to my roots pretty fast. Also, I learned the truth of the old saying, "I've been poor and rich, and rich is better!"

He got a hug from Sam and handshakes from Charlie and Nathaniel.

Nathaniel looked at his watch. "It's close enough to 4. Shall we have our meeting?"

Sam fired up the digital Kanban board. Since the break-in, they'd taken to only waking it from the screensaver when they were using it.

"Terry, you first. We're all dying to know what you found," said Nathaniel.

"Well, it seems Danny wasn't a bad kid. But he was small for his age and hung around older kids. One farmer told me that Danny was a wannabe, a tag-along, a follower. To prove himself, Danny would do what the older kids would egg him on to do. One kid, the old farmer said, was just plain evil. None other than our own Avery T. Wilson.

"No shit!" said Charlie.

"It seems that Danny got in trouble stealing a generator from a barn, which Avery had put him up to. But it was Avery who burned down the dilapidated barn. Despite its condition, the farmer who owned the barn didn't appreciate it, and his cousin was the circuit court judge. He put Danny on a year's probation, but to get Avery out of town, the judge offered him a one-way ticket to the Marine

Corps recruiter's office and eventually a paid trip to Iraq and Afghanistan.

"As the story goes, Avery turned out to be a ferocious soldier, fearless. He earned many medals and promotions that eventually took him back to Quantico with the lieutenant he'd served so well so many years ago: General Wesley Mathers."

"No shit," said Charlie.

"I went to talk to the local sheriff, a good old boy if ever I've met one, talking about their local war hero. But I saw his Black deputy had different ideas, so I had a beer with him—Joshua Francis. According to Francis, Wilson runs into Bode on a trip home to, and here I quote, 'strut around town in his uniform' a few years ago. Bode's wife had just left him, taking their three kids, and he was in a bad place.

So, Wilson helps him get the FBI job. According to Francis, such a generous gesture was out of character. He was sure Wilson had ulterior motives for doing so."

"Would that be the possibility of a sideline in cheap auto repair?" asked Nathaniel.

"That was my thought too. I'd bet you money that Wilson was taking a cut. Francis stayed in touch with the families to keep abreast of Bode and Wilson—especially Wilson—making sure he'd be prepared if, and I quote, 'If that little psycho ever comes home.'"

"Terry, this is all great work. There's no doubt that Wilson is involved in this, and this is proof of a connection to Bode."

"Speaking of Wilson," said Sam, "he asked me about the break-in. I brushed it off but confirmed we had one."

"Now that's interesting," said Charlie. "Bode's deputy, Eddie, said something similar about Danny being a follower. It seems he'd been taking a boatload of calls on his cell in a car in the parking lot these last few months. Someone called T."

"Very interesting. Ok, what else do we have?"

Charlie said, "As soon as we got the autopsy report with the green fiber, I contacted the PX about any bulk purchases, anyone who might have purchased three NA green polos and three pairs of shoes of various sizes. The guy who runs the PX told me that there were a lot of purchases for a couple of weeks before the murder because a new NA class came in and bought out the store to get ready."

"Yes, but the shoes, in particular, might constitute a unique pattern with two size 12s and one size 9," said Sam.

"I pointed that out, but the guy was swamped and said he'd keep checking but was going through receipts manually. However, I did ask one of the analysts from SIOC to see what he could find going through the inventory system of the PX. And bingo! On September 1, the Academy PX had a cash purchase for 3 T-shirts—one medium and two large, and three pairs of shoes: two pairs of size 12s and one size 9."

"That's great," said Terry. "Almost two weeks before the murder too. That speaks to premeditation."

"The cash thing makes it harder, but I've got another analyst working on any tours on that day at the academy. Still can't rule out any NA students, but if we find an interesting visitor, that might help a lot."

"Great work, Charlie. You know I'll have to eat a lot of crow with Reggie Samuelson at SIOC if this pans out, so I want to be sure before I sit down to some humble pie. Not to mention the Director!"

Then, Sam said, "I'm still on the trail of Rasheed's missing military file jacket. The archive told me it had been checked out to the Provost's office, but the Gunny there claimed up and down he didn't have it. To say I got a cool reception would be an understatement. It didn't smell right, so I'm backtracking with Saint Louis now. I'm also tracking down the guys Rasheed served with. But I'm treading carefully because I don't want to tip off Wilson that I'm poking around the Marines. He'll see that as a betrayal."

"Would it be better if one of us did it? A little good cop/bad cop?" asked Nathaniel. "Wilson already thinks I'm an asshole."

"That's interesting. Let me think about it. I checked with John in Behavioral Sciences, and he's thinking now that the 'little guy' in the assault was a psychopath or at least a sociopath by the pattern of the beating and its brutality, especially on the skull. Pretty personal. The other two chimed in, but the real damage was done by size nine."

"Interesting, because the older Black farmer who gave me a tip said that Avery was always considered a psycho. He'd tortured animals, bullied and had badly beaten up a few kids in school, done all kinds of shit before the Marine Corps."

Charlie asked, "So, what exactly is the difference between a sociopath and a psychopath?

"The same question I asked John." She pulled out a yellow pad with lots of notes. "John told me it was clinically complex, so he'd dumb it down for me." Nathaniel laughed. "Sounds like John."

"He said he sees three aberrant types in his work: narcissists, sociopaths, and psychopaths. They're all narcissists—go around bullying people, blaming others for any bad that happens to them, and are covering up for massive personal insecurity."

"Sounds like Trump!" said Terry, and everyone laughed.

Sam continued to closely read her notes: "Sociopaths and most antisocial personalities are narcissists who are fashioned by others around them to act out violence. So basically, sociopaths or antisocial personalities are made, not necessarily born. They're capable of doing almost anything that protects them. These antisocials possess a kind of superficial charm but lack truthfulness, sincerity, and even nervousness when causing harm to another. They are pathologically egocentric and possess no empathy or shame. A lot of actors and politicians have tendencies in this direction."

Nathaniel interrupted. "Reminds me of my courses in college in abnormal psych. Sociopaths start as delinquents who can go either way unless there's an intervention."

"Like become politicians or be forced into the military?" asked Terry.

"Precisely."

Sam continued, "Then we have the great white sharks of narcissists: the psychopath. These creatures, like Ted Bundy and the Green River Killer, can kill you in your house, make a sandwich, and eat it at your kitchen table while you lie in a pool of blood a few feet away. No fear, no remorse, no conscience. They do what they want if it benefits them. To hell with the rest of the world."

"So, we gotta assume that this guy isn't gonna have an attack of conscience and just confess," said Charlie.

"According to John, not bloody likely."

"Great work, everyone. Keep going. We don't have a motive yet, and we need one. Rasheed was a bit of a jerk, but that's not enough motivation for this murder. It took careful planning." There were nods all around.

"Ok, if nothing else, let's wrap up early today. A quick drink at The Boardroom to welcome Terry back?"

"Well, you did tell me to be visible, Nathaniel. This'll let the rumor mill know I'm back."

"An operational reason for a drink? That means it's on the Bureau, right boss?" said Charlie

"Naturally, Charlie. We have a research budget," said Nathaniel with a wink.

The Boardroom was pretty empty just before 5 pm, but a few heads turned as they walked in. Sam and Nathaniel went to the bar to collect the drinks as usual. As they waited, Sam got a text.

"Do nunneries still exist? The apps are awful. I hate you."

Sam laughed and texted back: "They do, but I think you have to be Catholic. I'm at the Boardroom with some colleagues—join us?"

"Something good?"

"Remember my friend I set up on Hinge?

"Yeah."

She just texted me to ask if nunneries still exist."

"Going that well, huh?"

"Want to guess how many unsolicited dick pics she's seen?"

"Ugh."

"The more I think about it, the more I want to introduce her to Charlie. I think it would be good for both of them."

"I love this plan. Can I help?"

"I'm counting on it. I thought I'd invite her here one night and leave them if it's going well."

"Good plan. They might need some training wheels. The last time Charlie was single, I think Lincoln was in office. Why not tonight?"

"That's a great idea. I'll text her. Ok, think you can handle the two pints?"

Nathaniel managed to stroll back over to their table with two pints in one hand.

"Good work, Sport. If this agent thing doesn't work out, you can always be a mediocre waiter."

Nathaniel grinned. "Always good to have a fallback, Charlie."

"To Terry's return!" said Sam, and everyone clinked glasses.

Sam's phone buzzed. She answered it and asked, " Is it OK if my friend Marge joins us? She just texted me."

"Sure thing. But I can only stay for one; my wife is thrilled about having dinner with me," said Terry.

"Enjoy it, Terry. Well, I got nowhere to be; spending too much time in that box at the dorm makes me feel like I'm going nuts."

"Wait, you're telling me not all adults live in dorms? Charlie, you're blowing my mind."

"I don't know how you do it, Sport."

Sam caught sight of Marge and waved her over.

"Everybody, this is Captain Margery Anton, USMC, my good friend and neighbor. Marge, this is my team."

Marge, dressed in jeans and a navy and white striped long-sleeve t-shirt, shook hands around the table. Sam, sitting next to Charlie, scooted over to make room.

"Margery with a G or a J?" asked Charlie.

"G. Why?"

"Your parents' big mystery fans? I love Margery Allingham."

Marge stared at Charlie. "Oh, my god. You are the first person I have ever met who guessed that!" Marge beamed at Charlie. Sam nudged Nathaniel with her foot, and he nudged her back.

"Let me get you a drink, Margery."

"Let me get it, Charlie. On the Bureau, remember? What'll you have?"

"It's Marge, please. A glass of white. Anything but chardonnay."

"No bourbon?" asked Sam in surprise.

"You know I love bourbon, but I miss having a fridge for a glass of chilled white."

"Coming right up. Anyone else?"

"I'll take another, Sport."

"Me too. Think you can handle three different glasses?"

"I'll give you the sign if not," said Nathaniel, tugging his earlobe.

"I'm teaching him the waitress carry," explained Sam.

"An important life skill."

"So, Marge, you live at the BOQ with Sam?"

"I do, for my sins. I'm recently divorced, so being back in dorm housing has been... an adjustment."

"I can imagine. I'm in the FBI dorms while I'm here, and I gotta tell you, I haven't slept in a single bed since college. I didn't miss it."

"On the bright side, I don't miss vacuuming either. And the neighbors are nice." She winked at Sam. Nathaniel arrived with the drinks.

Terry finished his wine. "I've got to head out. My wife expects me home for dinner. And in case I was tempted to stay, she told me it was lasagna. Marge, it was lovely to meet you."

"You too, Terry. Enjoy the lasagna."

"I will. I'll see the rest of you yahoos tomorrow morning."

"It's good to have you back, Terry," Nathaniel said.

"It's good to be back. Night, all."

"Speaking of dinner… shall we get some food?" asked Sam.

"Oh, let's. I could murder a burger."

"Tough day at the office?" asked Charlie as he passed out the menus.

"Let's just say I cannot wait for these confirmation hearings to be over. I'm honestly shocked we wrapped up as early as we did."

"So, you're just here until the hearings, Marge?" asked Nathaniel.

"Yup, then it's back to my regular job in DC."

"Everybody knows what they want? I think I just spotted the waitress," Nathaniel said as he waved her over.

"Hi, folks. What'll it be?"

"I'll have a cheeseburger, medium, regular fries. Oh, and can I have ranch on the side?" asked Marge.

"Sure thing, hon."

"I'll also have a cheeseburger, medium, no tomato, fries. Do you have malt vinegar?" asked Sam.

"Sure do."

"Hamburger for me, medium, sautéed onions, regular fries, and regular ketchup for me," said Charlie.

"Well, I was going to get a salad, but I hate to break the trend. I'll have a cheeseburger, medium rare, extra pickles, regular fries."

"You got it. Coming right up," said the waitress, and bustled off to another table.

"Charlie! Was that the diner waitress from Hogan's Alley the other day?"

"You know, I think it might be."

"What's Hogan's Alley?" asked Marge.

"It's the fake town where the FBI practices maneuvers. It's pretty cool. Charlie took me on tour on my first day when he was trying to figure out whether I was trustworthy."

Charlie blushed.

"I'd have done the same in your shoes, Charlie."

"Hogan's Alley sounds awesome. They have a real restaurant there too?"

"Yup, and the coffee is good. Cheap, too, cause you might get held up while you're getting it. Great excuse to be late for a meeting, though," said Charlie.

"Now that's one I've never heard before!" said Marge with a laugh.

"I'll give you a tour sometime if you like, Marge."

"I'd love that!"

"Better be careful, Charlie. You keep giving tours; they're not gonna let you leave."

"There are worse jobs. I know. I've had several of them. I was this one's training officer, for instance."

Nathaniel put a dramatic hand on his chest. "I was a model agent! You wound me, Charlie."

"Nah, you were alright. Good instincts, but you'd only seen the fancy side of life. Not like some of these knuckleheads they sent me. Christ on a bicycle."

"Here you are, folks," said the waitress as she delivered the burgers. "Anything else I can get you?"

"No, I think we're all set. Thank you," said Nathaniel.

Sam elbowed him. "You were watching her technique, weren't you?"

"It's impressive!"

"You have to walk before you can run, grasshopper. If you get the drinks, I'll teach you plates."

"Oh, plates will be a cinch for him!" said Marge. "Look at the size of those hands." She eyed Nathaniel critically. "Rower?"

He grinned. "Guilty." He turned over his palm to show his callouses.

The conversation lagged as they dug into the burgers.

"Ok, Miss Malt Vinegar, where did you learn to eat fries the British way?" asked Charlie as he dipped a fry in thoroughly American ketchup.

"I went to Annapolis on a soccer scholarship. The summer between my junior and senior years of high school, I went to England and played in a youth league. It was an absolute blast. We played at Tottenham Hotspur's stadium most of the time. I learned to eat chips the English way, drive on the other side of the street, and sneak into a pub. I almost stayed. I got recruited by one of the women's teams, but I was homesick for California by then. I wasn't ready to leave home yet and move a continent and an ocean away. But the offer to stay in London made convincing my mom to let me go to the naval academy much easier."

"Your dad didn't object?" asked Nathaniel.

"Nah, he was a retired Navy officer. I grew up in Monterey because he taught there at the Naval Postgraduate School. He was thrilled. But my mom found navy life hard. I think she was worried it would be hard for me. Of course, there's a huge difference between being a naval officer and a navy wife."

"Ok, Marge, what's with the ranch dressing?" asked Nathaniel.

"I'm from the Midwest. I love ranch. End of story." Everyone laughed.

"Where in the Midwest? We gotta stick together with these coastal elites," said Charlie as he gestured to Sam and Nathaniel.

"Michigan. I'm from Dearborn. Grew up in one of those Henry Ford bungalows."

"And here I thought we were getting along so well."

"Oh no, you're not a Buckeye, are you?"

Charlie pulled his wallet from his back pocket. It was bright red, with the Ohio State logo stitched in white. Sam dipped a fry in vinegar and then rapid-fire texted Nathaniel under the table.

Shit. Did you know there was an Ohio/Michigan thing??

Are you kidding? I don't know a damn thing about college football. Stanford doesn't play anyone west of Utah!

Sam watched the banter between Charlie and Marge as they rehashed last year's game. Both were gesturing wildly, the remains of their dinner forgotten.

"The Romeo and Juliet thing seems to be working," said Sam quietly.

Nathaniel leaned closer. Sam could smell his cologne, sharp and fresh and piney. She remembered the feel of his lips on hers but forced herself to focus. "Should we leave it?"

"Let's get one more round. I don't want to ruin the moment by leaving."

"Another round, guys?" Nathaniel asked the table.

"I'm in," said Sam.

"I'm gonna need it if we keep talking football," said Marge, draining her glass.

"You're gonna need it?" Charlie said in mock indignation.

"I don't see our waitress," said Nathaniel, craning his neck. "Sam, give me a hand?"

"Sure thing."

As soon as they were away from the table, Marge put her hand on Charlie's arm. "Put a pin in it, slugger. Is it just me, or is something brewing between our companions?"

"What? Oh, yeah. For sure. Nathaniel should be so lucky. But he's technically her boss, so he's unlikely to make the first move."

"I thought he was a rule breaker! Damnit."

"Oh, he is. But he's also a good guy. He'd never want to make a woman he worked with uncomfortable."

"Ok. I guess we have our work cut out for us then."

"What?"

"Keep up, old man. You want those two to be happy or not?"

The implications of A, spending more time with Marge, and B, seeing two people he liked very much happy, snapped into place in Charlie's mind. "Ok, what's the plan then?"

"Here they come. Give me your number, and I'll text you later."

Charlie's stomach did a little flipflop as he gave Marge his number. He couldn't remember the last time that had happened.

As the evening wound down, Sam glanced at her watch. "Oh shit. I hate to break up a party, but I turn into a pumpkin soon."

"We should all get some sleep. Big week ahead," said Nathaniel. He downed the last of his beer. "Marge, it's been a pleasure."

"Thanks for letting me tag along—this was a blast. I can't wait to see Hogan's Alley."

"You let me know. Happy to play tour guide."

"Well, gents, see you tomorrow," Sam said as she stood up. "You ready, Marge?"

"You bet. Night fellas."

Outside, the air had turned crisp. "Brr, should've brought a jacket," said Marge, rubbing her arms.

"We can walk briskly. So, did you give your number to Charlie? You two seemed to hit it off."

"I did! I liked him, even if he is a Buckeyes fan. And if you planned to set me up on Hinge to make Charlie seem even more attractive, it worked."

"Marge! Of course not. But I like you, and I like Charlie. And I like to see people happy."

"How about you and James Bond there? He's smitten with you."

"And he's also my boss. Technically."

"True. But he won't be your boss forever."

"I'll say. Since I may or may not have kissed him last night."

"SAMANTHA! You dark horse. Tell me everything."

"We were sitting on a bench in front of the Academy. But I told him that had to be it until he was no longer my boss. Sometimes being a rule follower is the worst."

"You better hurry up and solve this case! I bet that man has a very nice bathrobe." Their laughter echoed off the buildings into the crisp night sky.

18
CLEAN UP

Tuesday, September 23

The following day, when Charlie got out of the shower, he had a text from Eddie, Danny's deputy, at the garage: Have something for you. He texted Nathaniel to let him know what he was doing, grabbed a coffee and a muffin from the mess, and set off for the garage. Eddie was sitting at Danny's desk in the bullpen when he arrived. In front of him was an olive-green military ammo box, often used by Marines as storage after their official use. Hunters buy them at Army surplus stores as macho mini-storage containers—think steel-cased Tupperware for warriors!

Eddie looked up at Charlie and said, "Hey, Charlie. I didn't know what to do. Started to look through the Buick because Danny's wife wanted to sell it. I told her I'd clean it up. I saw Danny writing stuff in the car; then he'd put something in the trunk. But I didn't think anything of it. When I opened the trunk, I found this box pushed back in the corner under a green wool blanket. Felt like I was breaking and entering because I didn't have a warrant."

"You don't need one, Eddie. You're a civilian. And you can legally turn it over to me, whatever it is."

Eddie pushed the olive-drab box across the desk to Charlie. It looked more like an industrial lunchbox than anything, except for the mustard-yellow stenciling that said: 200 Cartridges 7.62MM–M13, along with some other inventory coding. Charlie carefully opened up the end latch and looked inside. There was a Walmart bag, which Charlie took out and opened to find two burner cell phones. Charlie almost missed a small black notebook sitting quietly and unassumingly on the bottom.

"Thanks, Eddie. I'll take this stuff back to the team. If you find anything else, let me know. And be careful."

"I will. I got no intention of hanging off a tow arm."

Charlie stuck his head in Nathaniel's office when he got to the office. "Eddie found some stuff in Danny's trunk. Might be something, might be nothing. But I've got two cellphones and a notebook to go through."

"Great work, Charlie."

At 12:30, Terry stood up from his desk. "I'm ready for lunch. You guys ready?"

"Yeah, and I missed your complaints that this food is such a far cry from the haute cuisine of your law firm dining room."

"Don't listen to him, Terry. Poor Charlie had to find something else to grumble about with you gone." There was much laughter as they headed for the door.

Some days they quietly talked about the case, but most days, the conversation was casual and a welcome break from work. After they'd ordered, Sam proposed a topic, as was her way. "OK, favorite TV, Netflix, Hulu, or whatever series. I'll start. I love *Veronica Mars*. It ran for three seasons on the WB, back when that happened. It's a high school-set noir starring Kristen Bell. It's fantastic."

"Didn't it just come back on Netflix?" asked Terry.

"Yeah, but the new series was disappointing. There was also a movie a few years ago, which was awesome."

"That sounds like a movie I saw years ago called Brick. It was also a noir set in high school. My wife picked it for movie night, and I rolled my eyes, but it was really good."

"I'll have to add that to my Netflix queue. What about you, Nathaniel?"

"There's an incredible British show called *Line of Duty* about an internal affairs division. Each season is a different investigation. That show does tension like no other. I got hooked on it on a Virgin Atlantic flight a few years ago. Whenever a new season comes out, I block off a weekend—binge the whole thing."

"So, Terry, now that you've stopped complaining about the food, what's your favorite series?"

"*Luther*," Terry said without hesitation. "Idris Elba is brilliant as DCI John Luther. Nothing else comes close for me."

"Yes, I agree with the quality," replied Nathaniel, "and how well Idris plays off against Ruth Wilson in that series—written by Neil Cross. But Luther over Stringer Bell from *The Wire*? I dunno."

Terry put down his fork and said, "Ok, that's not fair. Don't make me choose!"

"Did you know the show's creators on *The Wire* didn't know Idris Elba was British when he auditioned? He came in doing the Baltimore accent. They didn't know until they called to offer him the part," said Sam.

"Isn't that amazing? When you hear how thick his London accent is, you can see why he did it that way."

"And last, but by no means least, Charlie."

"I'm a fuddy-duddy, but I love a good western and a tough sheriff. My favorite is *Longmire.* Walt Longmire is the sheriff of Absaroka County in Wyoming."

"What a great series," Sam replied. "I like Lou Diamond Phillips as Henry Standing Bear, owner of the Red Pony and continual soiree. Have you read the books? They're even better."

Charlie looked at her and said, "When do you find time to sleep? You're up on all the shows."

"That's classified, Charlie, "Sam said as she winked at him. "I fly a lot for my job. I find it hard to sit still for a long time unless

I'm really into a show. The ability to download a Netflix show to your device was like Christmas morning."

After lunch, they headed back to the office. Terry was busy inputting everything he'd learned from North Carolina into CaseMaster. Sam checked her email to find she'd finally received the National Academy front desk sign-ins and swipe-ins. She immediately downloaded the excel files and began sorting them. A couple of searches later, she leaned back in her chair. "Well, well, well."

At 4 PM that afternoon, the team huddled up near the electronic whiteboard toward the rear of the office. Nathaniel led off. "I humbled myself today for the good of the team," he said. "Called Reggie Samuelson and thanked him for his analyst's good work. I could feel him gloating on the other end of the phone." There was a round of polite applause, and Nathaniel took a bow. "Sam, what do you have?"

"I finally got the files from the NA. I checked the front desk for any unusual sign-ins during the week before and the week after the start of Rasheed's class to see if there might be a pattern worth following. Nothing in the sign-in list."

Nathaniel said, "Thanks—"

"But, wait, there's more, as they say in the movies. I decided to check scans into the Academy. And bingo: Avery T. Wilson and two guests came in a few days before the NA check-in for Rasheed's class. It's still not a slam dunk, but the circumstantial evidence is piling up."

"Great work," said Nathaniel.

Terry said, "Well, I started to look into our General Mathers. He's quite the boy scout. But I'm digging—my firm has a bulldog investigator. So if this guy got so much as a speeding ticket, we'd know. He's almost too clean, you know? My Spidey sense is tingling."

"Spiderman! Even I got that one," said Charlie. Everyone laughed.

"It goes against everything I know to use an outside investigator on this, but we can't afford to tip Mathers or Avery off," said Nathaniel.

"Agreed. Terry, is your investigator like Kalinda on *The Good Wife*?" asked Sam.

"Aside from not being a tiny Indian woman, he's exactly like that." Sam laughed.

Finally, with dramatic effect, Charlie pulled out the ammo box. He plopped it on the desk and opened it. "I got this from Eddie in the garage. It was hidden in the old Buick in the lot that Danny used as a private office." He reached inside and took out the bag with the cells in it. "Only one of the phones had been used; I guess the other was a backup. There were 18 calls to one number over the past several months. It was another burner, but Sam did something with the metadata, and we got a name."

"Please, Oh Lord, let it be Avery Wilson," said Terry.

"Bingo!" said Charlie, and everyone applauded.

"Now that's some concrete evidence right there!" said Nathaniel.

"The burner phone Danny called was in the same place as Wilson's cell 80% of the time. So either he was using it, or a ghost is haunting him with a cell phone," explained Sam.

"To quote my esteemed colleague," Charlie said, looking at Sam, "But wait, there's more."

Charlie opened the small black notebook with "Hunting Journal" printed on the cover.

"This was Danny's hunting journal. Pretty typical for avid hunters to record things like the date, weather, time, location, highlights, and other specifics about the hunt, including the species—deer, rabbit, duck. Most of the entries were like that in Danny's journal. However, about six weeks ago, he started to make notations about meeting up with 'T.' Think we all know who that is by now. "

"Does he ever refer to him as Avery or Wilson and connect him to T?" asked Nathaniel.

"Not really, but it's clear. We know Wilson got him the job at the FBI garage a few years ago, and Bode was grateful. But it seems that Wilson was calling in some debts. There are a few notes mentioning 'T' until about three weeks ago. That's when—and I quote: 'T asked me to help him on an important matter. Turns out some FBINA student from Detroit is trying to blackmail him. Asked for my help.' There were a few other entries about the Detroit cop blackmailing T, about T's boss, the General, about scaring off the cop. But the big one came on the morning Rashid was killed: "5:15 am—R runs out the gym door. Called T. Said he'd take it from here."

"Bingo," said Terry.

But Nathaniel said, "Not so fast, Terry. We've got a lot of circumstantial evidence and even motive, but many hearsays and innuendo-type cell phone calls from one burner to another. We have no connection between T and Wilson beside his middle initial. There is no physical evidence except some green fibers that could have come from any of the 250 other National Academy students. An old farmer in North Carolina said that Danny and Avery were connected. Not exactly the stuff we can get an indictment on, as much as we all want it. We need more direct evidence to make an arrest warrant stick. How about the other two who participated in the crime? Two big guys close to Avery. If we can figure them out, we can take a run at them. "

☆

Inside a motel off Route 1, just south of the base, with a vacancy sign that was only half lit up, Sgt. Major Avery Wilson's uniform was slung over a scuffed desk chair. Propped up on the bed in his olive-green Marine Corps-issued shorts and tank top, he drank straight bourbon from a half-empty bottle. Next to him sat a young woman in her bra and panties. She was Asian, petite, and timid—Avery's favorite type. His cell phone rang, and he grabbed it off the bed table.

"Hey, Mittens," said Wilson as he got off the creaky bed and headed into the bathroom to take a leak. "Shit's heatin' up. Need to see you tonight," he said, adjusting himself.

"Can't tonight. Goin' out with my new captain. Wants to get all buddy-buddy."

"Blow off that Naval Academy fag."

"But..."

"It's just SIX fucking days 'til the General's hearin' on the 29th. Meet me at the chapel parking lot at 23 hundred hours, Marine."

"Roger that, sarge. See you then."

Wilson emerged from the bathroom. The young prostitute had moved to the end of the bed. He charged at her like a wild boar, lifted her by the throat, and glared at her with venom in his eyes. "You fucking slope. What the hell are you listening to?" He pushed her up the bed toward the headboard. He grabbed the bourbon and threw down a couple of deep slugs. Then he staggered a bit as he slammed down the bottle and moved in on the girl. She cried, and he slapped her hard. "Shut the fuck up," he spat out.

Later that night, Wilson was parked behind the chapel, waiting as Romney pulled up in his marked MP car. He pulled up alongside Wilson, driver-window-to-driver-window, so both could stay in their cars and talk. The conversation got animated almost immediately. Wilson dominated it, and it ended as fast as it began.

Wilson peeled out, kicked up dust, and weaved down the road. Romney sat there in his car for a while.

19
HARDBALL

Wednesday, September 24

Early morning on the following day, Nathaniel drove down Route 95 on the hot lanes north toward Washington. Traffic moved well, and he was going around 70 and listening to the radio. "It's a beautiful September 24th in the Metro DC area. And here's the latest from the news desk."

The reporter's voice was muffled as a call came over the FBI radio. "Signal 10217, what's your ETA to the Director's office?"

"About 9:00."

"Roger that, 9:00. Out."

Nathaniel put back the radio mic. But as he looked into his rear-view mirror, he saw a dark sedan pull up at great speed behind him. WHAM! Suddenly, Nathaniel felt the jolt as the driver, in sunglasses and a plain baseball hat, pushed him from the rear. Nathaniel felt the car skid as he grabbed the wheel with both hands, struggling to keep his car on the road. Then the car behind him let off the gas and pulled even with the passenger's side rear quarter panel of Nathaniel's car. He employed a technique used by cops in high-speed chases to stop reckless speeders: pushed him from the right back side. Nathaniel's car fishtailed all over the road like a bass flopping on a boat deck, and he eventually did a 180 spinout and found himself in the median, looking south from the northbound lane. Even with his training and a high-performance vehicle, the technique had worked.

The other car had sped off when he was in complete control again. Nathaniel banged his hands on the steering wheel and looked to see if he could catch the rear plate on the sedan, but there wasn't one. He watched in his rearview mirror as the sedan swerved across two lanes of traffic to the next off-ramp, almost causing two other cars to crash. After catching his breath and breathing deeply, Nathaniel called Charlie.

"Charlie Thompson."

"Where are you? You sound like you're at the bottom of a tin can."

"I'm trying to shave and talk to you simultaneously. You're on speaker. What's up?"

"Well, you better put the razor down."

"Ok. You're making me nervous, Sport."

"I'm fine, but some joker in a black Ford sedan just tried to push me off the road. I'm speaking from the median."

"Jesus Christ!"

"I'd bet money it was one of our guys. He bumped me from the rear, got on my left side, and pushed my rear quarter with his car. Classic cop maneuver."

"Shit. This is getting serious."

"Yeah, we gotta solve this quick. That asshole owes me a new bumper. Can you call it into the duty agent? I've got a prayer of being on time for the Director."

"Sure thing. Any other details?"

"Guy had a plain black ballcap and big reflective aviators. No rear plate on the car either."

"Ok, got it. I'll report it to the duty agent at Quantico for the record. Drive safe, Nathaniel."

"I'll see you back at the office." Undaunted, Nathaniel continued toward DC and the J. Edgar Hoover Building. However, he did check his rearview mirror more often than usual.

At precisely 9:00 AM, Nathaniel was ushered into the Director's office, where she sat working. When she saw him enter, she motioned him to the hot seat—the chair on the left of her desk. If the Director were a gambler, her tell was the left-seat gesture. Nathaniel prepared himself for an old-fashioned ass—chewing. But to head it off, he held up his hand to stop her from launching into a tirade. It was a risky poker move, but he'd been to Vegas several times. "Director, I'd like to report an attempt on my life officially."

At first, she looked at him as if it were a joke, but he had on a poker face. "What the hell are you talking about?"

Nathaniel explained the ramming incident on his way up to DC. And he did so with a certain dramatic flair. "I was going about 70 and looked in my rearview only to see a black sedan doing about 90 come up and ram me in the rear end, no doubt to get my attention. And then he—assuming it was a he because he had a low-slung ball cap and sunglasses—pulled a high-speed law enforcement maneuver, causing me to fishtail all over the road. Thank God it was early; there were not many cars on the hot lanes then. After a 180-degree spin-out in the middle of the road, I recovered control of the vehicle and landed my car in the median facing south In the northbound lane. I don't mind telling you it was an exhilarating morning." Then he touched the band-aid on his forehead—the one he pulled out of the first aid in the trunk of his car for dramatic effect after he pulled into the Bureau parking lot.

"My God, Nathaniel. Are you OK?"

Mission accomplished, he thought to himself.

"I'm fine. It's true what they say about German engineering."

"I'm glad to hear it. So, update me on this most recent murder and where the investigation is. Clearly, you're making someone uncomfortable."

Nathaniel gave her a quick rundown on where things stood.

"It sounds like you're making progress. Do you need more people?"

"No, ma'am. I think we're getting close. But speaking of personnel… this is a bit awkward."

The Director looked at him over her glasses and raised her eyebrows.

"We've had a couple of break-ins at our office. Nothing was taken, just some papers rifled through. So, Charlie installed a small camera. Don't worry—no sound. And this is what we found." Nathaniel turned his phone so that the Director could see the video.

"Is that Jack Eller? Christ, what's he doing? I've half a mind to call Ralph Pelham and have Eller fired right now."

"I'd like to see how this plays out, Director, if possible. I think this little bit of leverage may prove useful."

"I know that look, Nathaniel, and you have something up your sleeve. Tread carefully, and don't do anything stupid. You know Ralph would love an excuse to tattle." Nathaniel grinned. "Now get out of here. And drive carefully."

After his conversation with the Director, Nathaniel drove back to the Academy without further incident.

When he returned to the office, it was clear Charlie had told Sam and Terry about his adventure. They both stood up from their desks when he walked in.

"I'm fine! I just need a new rear bumper."

"You sure you're ok? Because there's an easy joke to be made there," said Charlie with a laugh.

Nathaniel peeled the band-aid from his forehead. "This was a prop for the Director. I didn't hit my head. But I was lucky. I looked in my mirror and saw the guy coming at me, so I had a few seconds to react. We all need to be careful. Terry, are you sure I can't convince you to stay in the FBI dorm? Given what just happened, I don't like the idea of you going back and forth."

"I appreciate that, Nathaniel. Tell you what: I'll stay here sometimes. That should throw any pursuer off the trail."

"Great. And since we're pretty sure it's an inside job, it's not just on the road that we must be aware of. This was meant to rattle our cage, but I think it's time to do our own rattling."

"I agree, Nathaniel. They're getting nervous, so let's take advantage. What did you have in mind?" asked Sam.

"I want to go to Pelham's office and show him the photos from our surveillance camera. What we need is a link between Wilson and Pelham. I don't think Pelham has the guts to try something like pushing me off the road, so I want to see his face when I tell him."

"But what's your leverage? He will tell you he has no idea until he's blue in the face."

"He and the Director go way back, and her approval means a lot to him because he values his position. If he doesn't tell me the truth, I will tell him he leaves me no choice but to go to the Director."

"Good luck, Sport. You want company?"

"Thanks, Charlie, but this is better as a solo mission."

"Pelham's an appearances guy if memory serves. Put the band-aid back on your forehead," suggested Terry.

"A little visual aid," said Nathaniel with a smile.

"It's what I'd do if I were putting you on the stand," said Terry with a grin.

Less than an hour later, Nathaniel strode into Ralph Pelham's office.

"Nathaniel, what can I—"

"Ralph, someone tried to kill me today on my way to headquarters. And I want some answers right now."

"What! That's awful. How?"

"A dark sedan with no plates pushed my car off the road. Classic law enforcement maneuver. I think it was an inside job."

"I'm shocked and sorry but have no idea what the hell you're talking about."

Nathaniel pulled out a manilla envelope with several grainy but decisive photos of Jack Eller and thrust them at Pelham. He studied each one by one. Then he looked up at Nathaniel but said nothing.

"Now, YOU tell me why the hell Jack Eller broke into our offices."

Pelham looked like he was doing a complicated math problem in his head. He paused for several seconds, re-looked at several photos, and said, "I have no idea. But I will conduct—"

"Cut the bullshit now, Ralph. Jack Eller wouldn't take a piss if you didn't give him permission. So, stop it right now and tell me the truth. Or we can tell this story to the Director right now and let her sort it out." Nathaniel pulled out his cell and started to dial.

Ralph looked down at the floor, and Nathaniel read the shame on his face as though it were printed in giant letters. Pelham said in a subdued voice, "Put down the phone."

"OK. Start talking."

Ralph paused and looked up at the ceiling. Nathaniel noticed Ralph couldn't look at his face or look him in the eye. "I was told you had derogatory information on me. And that you were sending it to OPR."

"What kind of derog?"

"Racial stuff."

"Who told you that?"

Pelham hesitated. Did the math again. "Avery Wilson. He said you'd found some racial stuff on me and would send it to OPR. I panicked. But I swear I had nothing to do with anyone trying to push you off the road."

Nathaniel thought for a moment. Then he grabbed the photos from Pelham's desk and stormed out without another word.

20
TICK TOCK
Thursday, September 25

When Avery Wilson entered his office at 5:30 AM, he walked to the calendar on the wall next to his desk and crossed off September 24 with a black pen. An equal sense of relief and dread overcame him that something might happen before the 29th, circled in red. He hunkered down and flipped through the briefing book Marge Anton had pulled together for the General's Senate appointment testimony. As he paged through the tabs, he noted specific paragraphs with "WHAT?" and struck through others as if they were contaminated tissue, and he was exercising it. In the early morning, Wilson was the sharpest and most cruel—especially after his second cup of coffee.

Over the next hour, people trickled into the office, got coffee, and settled into what had become a command center of sorts with little doubt about who was really in charge despite the ranks on the uniforms. These days, the General worked almost exclusively from his home study, where the quiet helped him concentrate. Only Avery Wilson was allowed into the General's inner sanctum. When he did come in, it was to be questioned by Marge and several other lawyers to help the General prepare to be interviewed by the Senate.

The General, who had spent his entire adult life in an organization that respects hierarchy, was unused to the sometimes-aggressive tactics used by senators. Marge, who had been assigned the role of a hostile senator, found these sessions both nerve-wracking and exhilarating. In this morning's session, Marge would quiz General Mathers on his experience in Afghanistan. Marge expected it to be illuminating. So far, the general had remained calm under pressure. But it would be now if there was a chance to get under his skin. She sipped coffee, switched her uniform jacket for a civilian blazer, and said, "Jackson!"

"Yes, ma'am."

"I'm going to do confirmation prep with General Mathers. Hold the fort, would you?"

"Yes, ma'am. I'll have these statistics collated by the time you're finished."

"You're a whiz. Thank you."

With only days before the General's hearing, the office percolated with activity. Cell phones rang, texts dinged, copiers whirred, and people walked with purpose under Wilson's watchful eye. Time zipped by amid the focused activity. Soon it was 16:30, the time confidential trash pickup started. As was the custom, confidential trash was picked up by the corporal and taken to a large bin to be shredded later in the evening when the night duty security guard arrived at 20:00.

Marge was still working feverishly on Wilson's edits when the collection occurred.

"Anything to shred, ma'am?"

She waved off the corporal. "I'm still working, corporal. Thanks anyway, but I'll take it down myself later."

"Yes, ma'am."

At 5:30 PM, Marge was still working when Wilson left with a mock salute toward her. She nodded and bored back down into the briefing transmission document she was working on. "Oh, he did not try to correct my grammar!" fumed Marge. At 6:15, she sat alone, stretched, and yawned loud enough to be heard in the room's corners if anyone were there.

Marge walked around her desk, picked up the white-rimmed confidential trashcan next to her desk, and headed to the shredder. When she got to the large canvass hopper on wheels, she looked inside before tossing it in her trash. As Marge did, she noticed a document that had been torn into several pieces. A piece of the stationery on top bore the distinctive symbol of the 2nd Marine Division, which she'd become familiar with while assembling the General's briefing book. The handwritten document, the remnants of which had landed in a pile amid other documents, appeared to Marge to come from Avery Wilson's trash.

Out of curiosity, she pulled out the fragments, spread them out on a nearby table and started to put the puzzle together piece by piece. Jigsaws had always been her hobby, especially in the summer when she had more time to play as a kid. Like most puzzles, it took a moment to fit pieces together to get the picture. And when she did, she stood wide-eyed, looked around, scooped up the pieces carefully, and put them in her pocket. Because the trash run was not routine to her, Marge had forgotten the close-circuit television camera secreted on a rafter not far from the shredder.

When she left, a young corporal in the security office, who monitored the General's suite of rooms, picked up his cell and made a call.

As soon as she got back to her desk, she texted Sam. You home? I have something I need to run by you. Marge gathered her things, grabbing a roll of scotch tape from her top drawer. As she walked down the stairs, she felt her phone buzz. Sure thing. Bring Jack? Marge smiled and headed directly for the BOQ. She stopped at her room only long enough to change out of her uniform into jeans and a Marine Corps t-shirt. She knocked on Sam's door. "It's Marge."

"It's open. Come on in."

Sam sat on her single bunk so tightly made that she hardly made a dent in the olive blanket. The room was a compact, 10 x 10 cinderblock box with a private bath. Pretty spartan. Nothing was out of place. Normally Marge barged in and plunked down with abandon, but today she looked worried. She took a seat next to Sam on the bed.

"What's up, Marge?" Sam asked with concern.

Marge, busy putting the pieces together on the bedspread and taping them together, responded without looking up. "I pulled this from the office confidential trash. Pretty sure it came from Wilson's trashcan." She handed the scotch-taped letter to Sam. Before Sam read it, she asked, "How do you know it was from his trash?"

"Last in, first out."

"Thought that was only in accounting."

Marge laughed and said, "Yep, accounting and trash collecting."

Sam intently read the letter, looked up at Marge, and said, "Holy shit! This is Rasheed's original complaint letter from years ago, where he formerly complained about Staff Sergeant Avery T. Wilson and Lieutenant Wesley Mathers! The one he sent to Marine Corps Headquarters. Look at these two holes punched at the top of the letter. They must have taken it from his file. The one Romney said he never saw. Bullshit! It's the smoking gun we've been looking for. Great work, Marge. We gotta call Nathaniel right now."

"That's what I thought it was. But, Sam, if Wilson is involved in this, be careful. He's devoted to the general and will do anything to protect him. Anything."

"Well, someone tried to run Nathaniel off the highway this morning, so I'm already being careful."

"Holy shit! Is he ok?"

"He's mostly concerned about the damage to his beloved car. He's fine. But if they're lashing out, we're getting close."

"Well, I'm glad to hear he's ok. Be a crime for anything to happen to that beautiful face." Marge looked at her watch. "I'll be back in half an hour. I got to head up to my room to finish a few things for tomorrow. Then dinner? I'm starved."

"Sure, and Marge, thanks again. This is the piece we've been missing."

Marge gave a thumbs-up as she headed for the door. Sam dialed Nathaniel's number.

"Nathaniel? Guess what Marge found in the confidential trash. I'm sending you a picture right now."

Meanwhile, Romney drove his MP-marked car way over the speed limit as he and Wilson, riding shotgun, passed a sign that said BOQ—2 miles. Wilson kept hitting the dashboard to punctuate his rant. "Four goddamned days, and that stupid fucking bitch has to screw it up." Romney remained silent as he negotiated curves and narrow roads while he put the hammer down on the gas pedal.

Suddenly, another marked MP car pursued Romney, who turned on his red flashing lights. The trailing MP car dropped back to a regular rate of speed and discontinued pursuit. Romney turned off his flashers, gunned the car, and pulled up to the BOQ a few minutes later. Wilson hardly waited for the vehicle to stop before he vaulted out with Romney bringing up the rear. They exploded into the BOQ, galloped past the elevators and took the stairs two at a time. Wilson had his Marine K-bar knife in a sheaf on his belt. Romney had a gun in his MP holster.

Marge's room had the same spartan simplicity as Sam's, only more lived in. Some pictures and framed posters decorated the cinderblock walls. Propped up on her bed, Marge was making notes on another briefing document.

Wilson and Romney first tried the door, but it was locked. Then Romney slipped a master key from a ring of keys he'd brought from the MP's office into the lock and opened the door to a stunned Marge Anton.

"Sergeant Major. What's going on?"

Wilson walked right up to her and slapped her with his open hand so hard that her book flew. As she recoiled from the blow, he loomed over her.

"Where's the fucking letter?"

"What letter?"

Wilson cracked her hard again as he motioned to Romney, who grabbed her as Wilson yanked out his knife. Marge struggled against Romney, managing to jam her elbow hard into his gut. She felt his grip momentarily loosen, but Wilson stood right before her. "You bitch, you'll pay for that."

Wilson nodded to Romney, who pulled a handkerchief from his back pocket and stuffed it into Marge's mouth. Without blinking, Wilson sliced her right cheek, and blood streamed down her face and onto her T-shirt.

Marge's screams were muffled, and her eyes bulged as she pulled her head away, eyes wide open.

Wilson got within inches of her face. "Ready to talk now, bitch?"

She nodded.

Wilson pulled out the handkerchief and grabbed her by the throat. His eyes burned with white-hot rage.

Marge gasped for air like she'd been drowning and whispered, "Sam has it."

She cast her eyes down in shame, having given up her friend to stop her pain.

Wilson jerked her head up by her chin. "What room?"

"317."

Wilson nodded to Romney, who put the tape back over her mouth. Then Wilson stabbed Marge with a vengeance, and

Marge's eyes bulged in disbelief. She fell backward on the bed. Wilson cleaned off his knife on her T-shirt like he'd just finished carving a Thanksgiving turkey. They left with the same fury that they entered with, slamming the door. Marge lay there in shock.

Sam had just finished talking to Nathaniel about the letter. She was pacing around her room, thinking through the case, when she heard the empty BOQ room door next to her room bounce off the wall and a male voice shout, "Fuck!" Instinctively, she reached for the letter on the bed behind her and quickly stuck it out of sight between the mattress and the bed, punched "Nathaniel" on her cell's "Favorites" and stuffed it into her bra. Seconds later, she heard a key in the lock. As Romney and Wilson burst into her room, Sam turned in surprise. "Sergeant Major Wilson? What are you doing here? And Sergeant Romney. Who let you in? What's—"

Wilson charged her like a raging bull. He swung at her recklessly, and Sam dodged. But the room was small, and Sam could see Wilson was fueled by a rage so potent he could run through the cement wall and not even notice. She decided to bide her time and not try to fight her way out right then. She paused, and Wilson hit her with a punch that lifted her off her feet and hurled her onto the bed.

He pulled out his K-bar and put it within an inch of her left eye. She'd already started to bleed from the mouth.

"Give me the letter, or I shit you not, I will gut you like a fish," said Wilson, literally spitting out his words.

"I don't know what you're talking about."

Wilson's slap turned her head completely to the side. Then he grabbed her by the chin and yanked her around so he could stare into her eyes with a killer look and said, "Don't lie to me, bitch. Captain Anton tried."

"What happened to Marge? Is she all right?" Sam was careful not to say, "What did you do to Marge."

"Give me the goddamned letter, or you'll find out."

She closed her eyes briefly and sighed, "Under the mattress."

Wilson pushed her off the bed and lifted the mattress until it was vertical. He snatched the letter, inspected it, and said, "Now, we're all going to take a little ride." Sam grabbed the sweatshirt from the back of her desk chair and shoved her feet into her running sneakers.

"Downstairs, quietly. If you let out a sound, I will shoot you in the back of the head. Clear?"

"Absolutely." Sam had only seen a knife, but it didn't seem like a good time for questions. Outside her room, Wilson herded her towards the stairs while Romney headed back to Marge's room. Sam sent up a silent prayer that Marge was ok.

Outside, Wilson produced zip tie cuffs and bound Sam's hands in front of her. Then he opened the back door of the MP car. "Get in." Sam did her best to get into the car without falling. Wilson shut the door, and she took stock of her situation. Her hands were bound, but they were in front of her, and she wore good running shoes.

Sam heard the trunk open, and Wilson slid into the passenger seat. There was a big thump as Romney dumped something into the trunk. Sam looked at Wilson, but he stared straight ahead, fingers drumming impatiently on his knee. Sam sat bound and scared but waiting for her opportunity. She felt the calm that always descended on her in moments of stress, from penalty shootouts on the soccer field to coming under fire in Baghdad. Romney climbed into the driver's seat and pulled out leisurely, for all the world, like he was out for a Sunday drive.

About five minutes earlier that evening, Nathaniel had gotten Sam's call about having the letter that Marge had turned up in the confidential trash. And Terry had just stopped by Nathaniel's room before hitting the sack. “Terry, big news. Sam, or rather Marge, found us our smoking gun,” Nathaniel told him.

“What? That’s great! Tell me,” said Terry as he strode into Nathaniel’s room.

At that time, Nathaniel’s cell had begun to ring, and Sam’s name appeared. He answered, “Hey, Sam. You ok?” But what he heard back from the other end of the call made no sense at first: “Sergeant Major Wilson? What are you doing here? And Sergeant Romney. Who let you in? “ followed by a crash. Nathaniel quickly hit the mute button on his phone and turned to Terry, where his fear had been mirrored in Terry’s eyes.

Nathaniel blurted out, “No time to explain. Wilson is at the heart of this. I’m going over to the BOQ. Call Charlie and have him call Marge. I don’t have her number. “I’m going to keep the line open to Sam, so keep in touch by text.”

“Copy that. I’ll head to the BOQ, too, unless I hear from you.” Terry briefly clasped Nathaniel’s shoulder. “I’ll call the Director too.”

“No other—”

“No other law enforcement, I know. Go.”

“Thanks, Terry.”

Suddenly, Nathaniel and Terry heard coming from Nathaniel’s cell, “Give me the letter, or I shit you not, I will gut you like a fish.”

“Shit shit shit,” said Nathaniel as he sprinted from the room. Terry paused only to grab his car keys and then raced after him, dialing Charlie as he ran.

“Hey, Terry, what’s up?”

“Charlie, we have an emergency. Wilson is attacking Sam and maybe Marge as well. See if you can get Marge on the phone and meet me downstairs. And bring your gun.”

When Terry popped out of the elevator, Charlie was waiting for him.

“I can’t get Marge on the phone or text. There’s a chance

she's in the shower or something, but I don't think so." He looked worried.

Terry opened the task force door, made straight for the gun safe, and grabbed two nine millimeters and a box of hollow-point ammo.

"Your car or mine?" asked Terry as they headed for the parking-.

"Are you kidding? I have a Nissan Maxima from Enterprise. Unless you drive a horse and buggy, yours is faster."

"Copy that."

As they ran out to the parking lot, Terry tapped his remote as he ran. A silver Mercedes S class flashed its lights and roared to life.

"I'll say that's faster than a Maxima," panted Charlie as he threw himself into the passenger seat.

"I'll drive; you run coms. Do you know where the BOQ is?" asked Terry.

"Yeah. Take a right out of the parking lot." Terry shot a sideways look at Charlie.

"What? I walked Marge home after the tour of Hogan's Alley. I'm a gentleman." Terry grinned. "Left up here. This is a straightaway, so punch it." Terry did.

"Siri, text Nathaniel Croft."

"What would you like to say?"

"En route to BOQ."

"Your message to Nath—" Terry hit a button on his steering wheel, and the message was sent.

"I have got to get me one of these," said Charlie. "You don't even need me to run coms!"

"Siri, call Ann Greenburg. I told Nathaniel I'd let her know what's going on."

"Great, because I would also like to know what the fuck is going on."

☆

Nathaniel's timing was nearly perfect. Just as Romney's car pulled out at a sedate pace, Nathaniel screamed up in his BMW. He saw the back of Sam's head in the car, which shot adrenalin into his system. No sign of Marge, he realized. Romney saw Nathaniel's car and punched the gas.

"What the fuck, Romney!" growled Wilson as he braced himself on the dashboard.

"It's fucking Croft!" Since Romney had forced him off the road, he knew what that car looked like. "How did he know we were here?"

Sam kept her face neutral, but inwardly she breathed a sigh of relief that she'd hit redial as soon as she heard the door next to hers slam open. She braced herself as best she could.

"Who the fuck cares? Focus, Marine! Lose him." He picked up the radio. "This is alpha. We need backup."

Nathaniel hit the gas and chased Romney. The Charger was surprisingly fast, but it was heavy. The BMW's stick shift could have been a liability, but it was an asset in Nathaniel's expert hands. He used his hands-free system to call Terry on a conference line to keep the line to Sam alive.

"Nathaniel, you've got Charlie and me. The Director has been informed and is standing by. Where are you?"

By now, both cars were doing 70 in a 30-mile-an-hour zone filled with curves. The shrill sound of tire squeals blasted in the otherwise still night air.

"Chasing Romney, Wilson, and Sam in a marked MP car while doing about 70 through the base, heading roughly towards the golf course. No sign of Marge, but if she's alive, I bet she's in that car. It's a gamble, but I'd rather have you as a backup. What do you think?"

"We're on our way, Nathaniel. Punch it, Terry." Terry did.

"Keep the line open. I need both hands to drive."

They ripped through residential base housing, past the commissary, and through guarded gates without stopping, Nathaniel calling out the landmarks as they drove past. They hit barrels, went over curbs, and scared anyone in earshot as they roared through, almost out of control. A few minutes later, a second MP car roared up behind Nathaniel's car.

"Well, this just got interesting. There's another MP car behind me."

"And we're right behind him. If he wants to play bumper cars again, he's gonna have to go toe to toe with this hunk of German engineering." The four cars, conga-line-style, chased each other at speeds of over 80—skidding and curling along back roads like a snake on scalding desert sand.

Suddenly Romney's vehicle took off on a service road leading up to the golf course. The cars roared across the first fairway just as the sprinklers came on and then onto a secluded access road leading to a maintenance area on the base.

"Nathaniel, how close is the follow car to you? I can hit him, but I don't want to wreck you."

"That's a negative. He's right on my ass. Wait for my signal."

"Copy."

"Ok, I see a curve ahead. I'm going to make my move on Wilson. Terry, can you bump this asshole off? I'm done being the cream in this Oreo."

"Copy that," said Terry, forcing his way up next to the MP car.

"Brace yourself, Charlie." Charlie nodded, and then Terry wrenched the wheel to the left. The piercing sound of metal on metal was almost deafening, but Terry kept the pressure on, pushing the rear of the MP car off the road. Suddenly, the MP car tipped off balance, its left two wheels spinning in the air over the deep drainage ditch that ran along the shoulder.

"Take that, asshole!" shouted Terry as he straightened the wheel and roared past the MP car.

"Fucking right, Terry!" shouted Charlie as he thumped the dashboard. "Nathaniel, one MP car down. We're right behind you." Charlie turned around at a loud crunch. The MP car had tipped into the ditch, its top crushed by an ancient pine.

"That car is on its side in the ditch. That asshole isn't going anywhere for a while."

"Great work, guys. Ok, I'm going to force the lead car off the road. You guys ready? Things could get hairy after this."

"We got your back, Nathaniel. Let's end this."

As Romney's car slowed to negotiate a curve, Nathaniel sped up and thrust his bumper into Romney's rear quarter panel. Both vehicles started to fishtail off the road, hitting the undergrowth and creating a colossal crash worthy of any Hollywood blockbuster. Nathaniel's BMW broadsided a small tree. Romney's car crashed into the woods; a giant pine demolished the right-side front. Terry executed a neat e-break turn, putting his Mercedes broadside across the road, just behind Nathaniel's BMW and about 20 yards from the back of Wilson's MP car.

"Charlie, better exit out my side."

"Yah think?" replied Charlie, already crouching low in his seat, so his head was below the window. Terry and Charlie slid out of the Mercedes, keeping their heads well below the top of the car. It was dark, except for the lights from the mangled vehicles crisscrossing the woods. The sharp contrast made the scene look almost black and white.

"Nathaniel?" called Charlie softly. The BMW didn't look too bad, but car accidents could be deceptive that way. Just then, the driver's side window went down.

"Hey, guys. I can't open my door, and they've got a clear shot at me if I try to go out the window. Can you give me some cover?"

"You got it, Sport."

Charlie checked his weapon, chambered a round, and peeked through the rear windows. Wilson was nowhere to be seen, but Romney was on his feet, bleeding from the forehead and advancing on Nathaniel's car. "Shit," whispered Charlie. He rose up to brace his arms on the trunk in one fluid motion and fired two quick shots into Romney's torso. As he did so, he heard his old firearms instructor from new agent's training yelling, "center of mass!" Romney dropped like a sack of bricks onto the ground.

"All clear, Nathaniel."

Nathaniel's head and shoulders emerged from the window. He slid out headfirst, catching himself on his hands on the piney ground. Feet still in the air, a bullet crashed through the passenger window, nicking his leg.

Nathaniel crawled through the brush to Terry and Charlie and said, "Thanks, Charlie, you saved my bacon there for sure."

"You're welcome. You got a bit of a gash there, Sport," Charlie said, gesturing to Nathaniel's leg as Terry handed a loaded 9-millimeter to Nathaniel.

"Just a flesh wound. Nice driving, by the way, Terry." Just then, there was the distinctive sound of gunshots hitting the Mercedes.

"My wife always said this car would save my life, but I don't think this is quite what she had in mind," said Terry. "So, what's the plan?"

But before Nathaniel could answer, Wilson shouted, "Croft!" Wilson had pulled Sam from the back seat and put a gun to her head. Nathaniel sprang up and faced Wilson over the hood, with his gun pointed at him.

Wilson bellowed, "Drop the weapon, Inspector, or your girlfriend is dead."

"I don't think so, Sergeant Major. You're outnumbered. Drop yours."

"Cut the bullshit, sonny, and drop the weapon now."

Quietly, Nathaniel said, "Terry, got anything small and heavy I can throw?" Raising his voice again, he said, "Besides, Captain Melton can take care of herself. She doesn't need rescuing." Terry quietly grabbed his metal travel mug from the back seat and slid it into Nathaniel's hand.

"Hey, Wilson! Here's a present for you," he yelled as he threw the travel mug to Wilson's right, away from Sam. The travel mug caught the beam of headlights and glinted as it whirled through the air. It drew Wilson's focus, and he fired at it. The millisecond his attention shifted, Sam dropped down, kicked Wilson in the crotch, and rolled out of the way. Wilson grabbed his groin as pain shot up into his abdomen. He fired back in the direction of the Mercedes. Nathaniel spotted the muzzle flash and aimed for it, shooting three rounds rapidly. One hit Wilson in the chest, and he went down like a puppet with his strings cut.

Sam ran over to Nathaniel, Terry, and Charlie. Nathaniel gave her a big hug. "Are you ok?" he whispered against her hair.

She pulled back and smiled. "Aside from these zip ties and a few bruises."

"Let me help you with those," said Terry, who had pulled a multi-tool out of his trunk.

"Thanks, Terry. Wait, listen," she said, looking over Terry's shoulder.

From behind them appeared the bloodied MP who had been driving the third car. "Drop your weapon."

"FBI," Nathaniel said, waving his badge.

"Drop your weapon, now!"

"OK. I'm tossing my weapon." Nathaniel said as he threw a rock near his left foot, which landed with a soft thud in the pine needles.

"Put your hands up."

"Marine, this is Captain Melton. Everything's cool. You can

put your gun away. I'm here with three agents from the FBI."

"Yes, Ma'am. I will."

But as he stumbled into the wash of Nathaniel's car lights, he still had his pistol drawn and ready. As he limped closer and into the light, his nametag appeared:

Pvt. Wilson.

Unsteadily, the young MP raised his gun. Blood dripped from a gash on his forehead, and he was shaking. He was only 10 yards from where they stood, and the three provided a large target together. Charlie wanted to reach for his gun but feared any movement would set him off. Nathaniel was getting ready to charge, and Terry was thinking about it too. But it was Sam who acted. Keeping her head low, she took a few steps and executed a neat slide tackle. The MP fired, but all he hit was the pine boughs overhead. Sam quickly rolled him onto his stomach and cuffed him. All the fight had gone out of him.

"He's not going to give us any trouble. I can't believe that little shit got the drop on us!" said Terry.

"Jesus, Sam, that was a hell of a risk you took," said Charlie as he helped her up.

"I knew one of you would try it, and I'm smaller and faster. But right now, we've got another problem. I think Marge is in the trunk of that MP car."

"Christ," said Terry, but Charlie was already sprinting across the clearing. He reached through the open driver's door to pop the trunk open.

"She's here! Oh shit, there's a lot of blood. " Oh no," said Charlie, peeling the blanket back from her face. Sam ran over, Terry rushed to get his first aid kit from the trunk, and Nathaniel pulled out his phone to call 911 and then the Director.

"Marge, can you hear me?" Charlie took one of her hands in his.

"Charlie?" Marge said weakly.

"I'm here, Marge. Where are you hurt?" Charlie asked as he gently brushed the hair from her face.

"Bastard…stabbed me. Shoulder."

Sam noticed she was clutching a pillow. "I think that pillow helped stop the bleeding. We better leave it. The blanket too."

"I've got a first aid kit. What do you need?" asked Terry.

"Marge, are you cold?"

"Cold."

"I've got hand warmers," said Terry, pulling them out and snapping them to life. Charlie gently tucked them around her.

"Nathaniel, where are we on the ambulance?" asked Sam, turning back towards him. He was still standing by the Mercedes.

"Should be… here…" And he slid down the side of the Mercedes, landing in a heap on the ground.

"Shit!" yelled Sam, running over. Terry was right on her heels with the first aid kit. She felt his pulse, which was steady, then noticed that his lower right pant leg was soaked with blood. "Give me your tie, Terry." She tied it tightly around his leg just above the wound. Nathaniel's eyelids fluttered as she pulled the tie tight. "Sam? Are you ok?"

"I'm fine. You probably passed out from loss of blood, you idiot. You didn't think to put a tourniquet on it? Don't they teach field first aid at Quantico? Jesus Christ. Now you've ruined one of Terry's best ties."

"That's a Hermès, Nathaniel," said Terry gravely. "But I've always hated that tie. Green's not my color." He grinned. "I'm going to go see how Marge is doing."

Nathaniel struggled to sit up, and Sam helped him lean back against the car. She sat down beside him, leaned over, and kissed him. When she pulled back, she said, "Don't scare me like that again, you absolute dickhead." Nathaniel grinned. "Can I tell you a secret? I hate the sight of blood. Always makes me woozy." In the distance, the scream of sirens approached.

21
IT'S A WRAP

Friday, September 26

Nathaniel lay in a hospital bed with an IV in his arm. His leg was bandaged and elevated on two pillows. Sam sat beside him, reading as he dosed in and out of sleep. Finally, he opened his eyes and looked over at her.

"What time is it?"

"Almost 10 AM. How are you feeling?"

"Like I just drank a six-pack of martinis. I haven't slept this late in years."

"The nurse said it was all the blood loss. Do you really get faint when you see blood?"

"Yup. Always have. How's Marge doing?"

"In stable but serious condition. She's got a nasty shoulder wound and lost a lot of blood. But being wrapped in that blanket and grabbing the pillow probably saved her life. Charlie's hovering over her." Just then, the room TV, tuned to CNN, showed an aerial view of the Quantico Marine Base. The text across the bottom of the screen read: Two Marines Killed in Gunfight with FBI.

Nathaniel said, "Hey, turn up the volume."

The camera switched to the studio, and a young woman anchor began:

"It wasn't Afghanistan or Iraq, but Quantico, Virginia, last night where three Marines tried to kill several FBI agents and two of their own, according to reliable sources close to the investigation. Sergeant Major Avery Wilson and Gunnery Sergeant Luther Romney were killed in a shootout with FBI Agents Nathaniel Croft, Terry Jamieson, and Charlie Thompson. Wilson's son, Private Jeffrey Wilson, was injured and taken into custody, and Marine Captain Margery Anton was stabbed and severely injured. Captain Samantha Melton received minor injuries while taking the younger Wilson into custody. The Wilsons and Romney were believed to be involved in an elaborate cover-up scheme. They are alleged to be responsible for the death of Black police officer and National Academy student Mohammed Rasheed and FBI employee Daniel Bode. Both crimes have drawn national attention. Sources report that Rasheed served with Wilson and Mathers in Afghanistan and was trying to block the Commandant appointee, General Wesley Mathers, who was Rasheed's platoon commander in Afghanistan. Details about the motive are still emerging, and we'll report them as we know more." The anchor paused and touched her earpiece. "This just in from Capitol Hill. Commandant hearings for General Wesley Mathers have been postponed indefinitely pending the outcome of the investigation concerning the Quantico incident between the FBI and the Marines."

"Wow," said Sam as she turned to Nathaniel. "I can't believe it's all over."

"Everything but the paperwork," he said with a grin.

Marge was settling into a private room on the medical recovery floor a few floors away. Charlie introduced himself to all the nurses, ensuring Marge had everything she needed.

"Jesus, I'm glad to be out of the ICU. Maybe now I can finally sleep more than 20 minutes at a time."

"Here in recovery, we only poke you once an hour," deadpanned one of the nurses.

"How on earth did I end up with a private room?"

"The FBI Director called the hospital, and presto! Private room. She sends her best wishes, by the way," answered Charlie.

"And so do we," said a deep voice from the doorway.

"Terry! I can barely see you behind all that greenery."

Terry put the vase of flowers on the windowsill. "My wife picked these out. She sends her love and says, " When you're ready for some home-cooked food, let us know."

Marge smiled. Just then, Sam peeked her head in. "Room for two more?"

"Two more?" asked Charlie.

"I just got discharged," said Nathaniel as he swung into the room on crutches. Terry pulled over a chair for him.

"Sport, are you wearing... sweatpants?"

"Don't laugh! My suit and Terry's poor tie were a total loss."

"I didn't like that tie. Good riddance!"

"Four visitors at a time?" said a tall, slender Black nurse with a strong Trinidadian accent. "Margery is here to recover. You best not tire her out, or you'll have me to answer to."

"Yes, ma'am," said Charlie. The nurse looked at each of them, shook her head, and left.

"All the nurses have been great, but she's my favorite. I didn't feel it when she put my IV line in."

"We won't stay too long. You need your rest, and so does this one," said Sam.

"I feel fine," Nathaniel said, stifling a yawn.

"Sure. Which is why the discharge nurse gave me strict instructions to take you right home."

"Via the office."

"No."

"No?"

"You're not my boss anymore," said Sam with a grin.

Nathaniel took her hand. "Thank goodness."

☆

The Hall of Honor at the FBI Academy commemorates lives given in service by FBI employees. Some were shot, some were blown up, and others were exposed to toxins associated with 9/11. Some are agents, others technicians, but all are heroes who will never be forgotten. Their photos were placed on the Wall of Honor, which new recruits and veteran agents walk by daily. Today, this hallowed ground would commemorate the bravery of some modern-day FBI heroes who survived and, luckily would not find their faces on this wall—at least for now.

Seated in folding chairs were about 50 people, with another 70 or so standing in the background. The podium at the front of this cavernous circular room had the FBI seal displayed on it. As the Director moved toward the podium, the room grew silent in respect for her office. Ann Greenburg was elegant in her dark tweed suit accented by a gold necklace and a gold-and-silver Yurman bracelet. Nathaniel, Sam, Charlie, Terry, and Marge sat next to the podium. Nathaniel had crutches by his chair, and Marge's arm was in a sling. Noticeably absent was Ralph Pelham, the Assistant Director of the Academy.

"I want to take this opportunity to thank some people today for an extraordinary job. First, to former agent Terry Jamison, who answered the call to return to duty. Terry left a lucrative DC law practice to rejoin the not-too-lucrative FBI for a temporary assignment." The crowd laughed, and she continued, "Terry put aside his, shall we say mixed feelings about the FBI to see justice done. " More laughter. "Terrence Jamison. I am pleased to present you with the Director's Award for Citizen Service, The Lou Peters Award, the highest award the FBI gives to a private citizen who helped the Bureau in its mission. Mr. Peters put his life in jeopardy to convict an organized crime boss, and after his death, was posthumously given the award."

The audience applause began and built as Terry walked toward the podium, his wife beaming from the front row. When he reached the podium, Terry stopped and faced the Director, who pinned on his medal and shook his hand.

"Next, Captain Samantha Melton was on loan to us from the Naval Criminal Investigative Service—better known as NCIS. Sam, your intuition and loyalty to the Navy, the Corps, and the Bureau were exemplary. I have the FBI Service Award and an open appointment letter to become an FBI Agent anytime you want in the next five years. According to a confidential source, I hear you have plans to leave the Corps."

Laughter and applause filled the room as Sam stepped forward to get both gifts. The Director pinned the medal to Sam's uniform, handed her the envelope, and shook her hand.

The Director adjusted her glasses and continued. "To Captain Margery Anton, who is still recovering from her near-fatal wounds, I present the Director's Award for Valor. Marge retrieved the pivotal evidence necessary in this case and was punished severely for doing the right thing." Charlie helped Marge stand, but she walked on her own to the podium, where the Director pinned on her medal. "Congratulations, and thank you, Marge." The Director led the applause.

"Next, I want to present the Director's Leadership Award to Special Agent Charles Thompson, our veteran agent in the Detroit office. Charlie's keen observations led to an early breakthrough, and he managed the vast amount of information in this case via the CaseMaster system. Inspector Croft said, 'Without Charlie Thompson, we all would have been lost. Charlie navigated all the details.' End quote. Charlie, in addition to the award, I officially transfer you to Quantico to help us with new agents and put you closer to a certain Marine captain. You can even give tours if you like."

Nathaniel led laughter and applause as Charlie approached the podium and accepted the award. The Director pinned the medal on Charlie's jacket, handed him the transfer letter, and shook his hand. When Charlie returned to his seat, he squeezed Marge's hand and smiled.

"Next, I have the pleasure of asking Inspector Nathaniel Croft to step forward or maybe to limp forward." Laughter came from the audience as Nathaniel came forward on crutches with help from Sam.

"Inspector Nathaniel Croft, by taking on this difficult case, you nearly sacrificed your life and your promotion to Special Agent in Charge. Nathaniel, I hereby give you the Director's Medal of Honor, the highest award I can confer for your Fidelity, Bravery, and Integrity above and beyond the call of duty."

Loud applause.

The Director stepped forward, pinned the medal on Nathaniel's jacket, and shook his hand. She then pulled out an envelope, handed it to him, and said, "I'd also like to introduce the new Special Agent in Charge of Hollywood—oops—I mean the Los Angeles Field Office." Laughter and applause. "Maybe a few words, Nathaniel?"

Nathaniel approached the podium mic and said, "Well, I don't know what to say."

"Now that's a first," Charlie said loud enough for the audience to hear.

The crowd roared.

"Touché. But I want to thank everyone on the team: Charlie, Terry, Sam, Marge, and the Director. The Director told me what she wanted and pretty much left me alone. Though there were some moments," he said as he raised his eyebrows, drawing a smile from the Director and a laugh from the crowd. "Also, thanks to everyone here at the Academy."

Cheers from the crowd.

"Now, it's off to Warner Brothers—the LA field office."

He winked and turned to Sam: laughter and applause. The Director retook the podium as Nathaniel returned to his seat and set down his crutches. She said, "Finally, it gives me great pleasure to introduce the new Assistant Director of the FBI Academy, Terry Jamison."

Genuine surprise swept across the faces of Nathaniel, Sam, and Charlie.

"Terry has always had a special interest in training since he sued the FBI!"

Laughter from the crowd. "Terry's agreed to an initial two-year appointment with the option to renew for as long as he'd like."

Terry approached the podium to loud applause.

After the ceremony, the team stood chatting. "How about one more lunch at The Boardroom?" asked Nathaniel.

"I've heard so much about it! I'd love to see it in person," said Eliza Jamison, Terry's wife.

"Well, that's settled then," said Charlie, taking Marge's good arm.

They were a slow-moving procession, but eventually, they were settled at a big table in the back. Once everyone had a drink, Nathaniel said, "I'd like to propose a toast: to the team who solved Quantico Kill. A more random assortment of people it's hard to imagine, but it turned out to be the perfect recipe. And that includes our unofficial members Marge and Eliza too. Cheers!" Everyone clinked glasses.

"Eliza, Terry tells me you insisted on putting such a well-equipped first aid kit in the car. The paramedics said it probably saved my life, so thank you," said Marge.

"Oh, Marge, I'm so glad it came in useful. Terry thought it was too elaborate, but once a Girl Scout..."

"Always a Girl Scout. Cheers to that," said Marge, and she and Eliza clinked glasses.

"So, Sport, when do you head to Los Angeles?"

"Once I'm fully recovered. Sam convinced me to take some vacation time, so we're going to do that too." He turned to grin at Sam.

"We're going down to the DR to sit on a beach. Someone tried to convince me that sailing from Massachusetts in October would be fun, but I'm done with ships for a while," said Sam.

"Did you put in your papers, Sam?" asked Marge.

"I did. Goodbye to the Corps, hello to the FBI. It was bittersweet, but I'm ready for a change."

"Marge, you'll be heading back to DC, is that right?" asked Terry.

"Yup. So long to the BOQ! I can't wait to get back to my condo."

"And I'll stay at Nathaniel's until I get my place. Turns out it's quite close to Marge," said Charlie with a grin.

"Eliza and I would love to have you guys over for dinner. Do you golf, Charlie?"

"Uh, no. But I do like a basketball game if you know a league for old men."

"I do, as it happens. But I wouldn't let them hear you say 'old men.' I've been meaning to get back on the court myself. Even with the commute to Quantico, I think I'll still have more time than I did as a partner."

"I'm not going to miss the BOQ, but I will miss having you as a neighbor, Marge," Sam said with a mock sad face.

"Ditto! We promise to come to visit. I've never been to Los Angeles."

"It's a fun town. And it'll give Charlie plenty to complain about." Marge laughed.

The waitress came over to take their order. When she got to Charlie, he said, "I'll have the chicken parm. Thanks."

"Charlie! No turkey sandwich?" asked Sam.

"Turkey and cheese will always be there. But it's time to try new things."

"To new things!" said Nathaniel, raising his glass.
"To new things!" said the team in chorus, clinking glasses.

ACKNOWLEDGMENTS

I want to thank a few people. First, my editor, Emily Murdock Baker, for making this book read so well. Her literary skills, for which I'm most grateful, far exceeded my expectations. Also, I'd like to thank Pio Juszkiewicz and Tom Rath for their confidence and support of my writing and willingness to publish my first novel, *The Manipulation Project.* Third, thanks to Daniel Kohan of Sensical Design for his expertise and patience in making the book look great. Finally, to my best friend and technical guru, Dean McIntyre, for using AI to create the cover and for listening to me through the journey of writing this novel.

Made in the USA
Middletown, DE
22 May 2023

31226505R00118